The woman repeated the question. 'What are you doing here?'

'What's it got to do with you?' Holly snapped.

'Are you Holly Adams?'

Holly stopped struggling.

'Are you?'

Holly nodded.

'Good,' the woman smiled. 'My name is Benson. P.J. Benson.'

Holly shook her head. 'No, you're not,' she said. 'You're nothing like P.J. Benson. I've seen her picture on the back of her books. And you look absolutely nothing like her!'

The Mystery Club series

Deceptions
The Mystery Club 12

Fiona Kelly

KNIGHT BOOKS
Hodder and Stoughton

Special thanks to Derek Farmer for all his help

A Catalogue record for this book is
available from the British Library

ISBN 0 340 60728 9

Typeset by Hewer Text Composition Services, Edinburgh
Printed and bound in Great Britain by
Cox and Wyman Ltd, Reading, Berks.

Hodder and Stoughton Children's Books
A Division of Hodder Headline plc
338 Euston Road
London
NW1 3BH

1 A secret meeting

'Jamie! Are you deaf?' Holly shouted. 'The phone's ringing!'

Normally Holly Adams would do anything to get to the phone before her younger brother Jamie. The last thing she wanted was him speaking to her friends.

He could be such an embarrassment. He didn't seem to realise that girls of their age weren't interested in computer games and football.

Especially Tracy and Belinda, Holly's two best friends and the only other members of the Mystery Club. They had much more important things to talk about. That's why Holly liked to get to the phone first. But just at the moment she was stuck in her bedroom.

'Jamie!' She tried again. Still no answer. *Typical*! she thought.

Holly began scrambling over piles of books. She had chosen the first morning of the holidays to rearrange her collection of mystery novels. The collection was vast and growing bigger all the

1

time. Usually it filled the shelves around her room but for the moment it was piled all over her bedroom floor.

Holly reached the door and swept the books that were blocking the way into a jumbled heap. The next moment she was racing down the stairs, her light brown hair bobbing as she went. As she reached the final step, the door to the sitting-room opened and Jamie shot out.

He grabbed the receiver. 'The Adams household. Jamie Adams speaking,' he said in a stupid voice.

Holly groaned with embarrassment and tried to take the receiver from him. But Jamie pulled a face and turned his back on her.

'Yeah!' he was saying. 'Yeah! . . . of course!' And finally, 'Wait a minute.'

Jamie passed the receiver over his shoulder. 'It's for you,' he told Holly.

'Who is it?' she whispered.

Jamie shrugged. 'I dunno. Vijay Jempson I think she said,' he called out as he disappeared into the sitting-room and slammed the door behind him.

Holly was puzzled. She'd never heard of Vijay Jempson. 'Sorry to keep you waiting,' she said into the phone. 'This is Holly Adams.'

'At last!' It was a woman's voice and she sounded irritated. 'I was beginning to think I'd got the wrong number. This is P.J. Benson.'

Holly froze.

2

'Are you still there?' said the woman.

Holly took a deep breath. 'I'm still here,' she said. 'Who did you say it was?'

'Benson. P.J. Benson. You wrote to me. Don't you remember?'

Holly certainly did remember. How could she forget? P.J. Benson was her favourite author. She wrote the kind of mysteries that had more twists in them than a bowl of spaghetti.

'So, do you remember or not?'

'Oh yes!' Holly gasped. Holly had written to P.J. Benson via her publisher some months before. But she had heard nothing back. In the letter she had told the author all about the Mystery Club that she had started with Tracy and Belinda, and about some of the adventures they had had together. She'd also asked if the writer would agree to be interviewed for *Winformation*, the school magazine.

'Well,' the woman continued, 'it so happens that I'm living near Willow Dale for a few months while I work on my next book. I thought we might meet up.'

Holly couldn't believe her ears. 'I'd love to!' she said. 'Where are you living?'

'That doesn't matter,' the writer answered. 'I keep my business and private lives quite separate. There's a hotel in Willow Dale called the The Queen's Head. We can meet there. This afternoon. Four o'clock. Can you make it?'

'Four? I think so.'

'Good. And, Holly, I value my privacy very much indeed. I don't want anyone else to know I'm in the area. So please don't tell anyone about our meeting. Don't even say you've spoken to me. If you do there'll be no interview. Do you understand?'

'Yes.'

'Fine! Four o'clock then.' And the phone went dead.

Holly stared dumbly at the receiver. She could hardly believe what was happening. Not only had she just spoken to P.J. Benson, one of the greatest mystery writers of all time, but a few hours later she was actually going to *meet* her.

How would she ever keep it to herself? Especially as the Mystery Club had arranged to meet at two o'clock that afternoon at the Willow Dale ice-cream parlour.

Holly replaced the receiver and ran back upstairs. On her bedside cabinet was a brand-new copy of *Fallen Angel*, P.J. Benson's latest book. Holly's mother had given it to her a few days earlier.

Holly turned the book over. On the back cover was a picture of the author. Smiling and silver-haired with a pair of round, horn-rimmed glasses, she looked like everybody's favourite aunt.

Funny, Holly thought. *She doesn't sound a bit like she looks*.

It was then that the first doubts entered Holly's

mind. What if it was all a trick? What if the person on the telephone wasn't really P.J. Benson? The voice certainly sounded younger than the photograph. But who would want to play a trick like that on her?

The only people who knew that Holly had written to P.J. Benson were Tracy and Belinda. And they wouldn't play a joke like that on her. Not her two best friends. Would they?

Oh, well, Holly thought. *I'll soon find out. If it is them, they'll never be able to keep quiet about it.*

By the time Holly had caught the bus into Willow Dale and walked through the streets to the ice-cream parlour, she had convinced herself that the phone call from P.J. Benson was genuine. Her only worry was how to keep the secret from her two friends.

As she walked through the door, Holly could see Tracy and Belinda sitting at their favourite table. Usually Belinda would be at least five minutes late for any meeting but when ice-cream was on offer it was different.

Tracy, dressed in a new lilac and grey track suit, was looking through the menu trying to decide what to order. But Belinda, who looked as though she'd come straight from mucking out her horse, was already tucking in. 'C'mon over quick,' she called as she spotted Holly. 'I've got something to tell you.'

As Holly threaded her way through the tables, she thought what a strange pair they made. Tracy, fit and active, with her short, blonde hair and ever-ready smile wouldn't have looked out of place in California. Which, after all, was where she'd lived until her parents divorced and her mother returned to Willow Dale. Belinda, on the other hand, was heavy and ungainly. Her untidy mousey hair and battered wire-framed spectacles would have had most girls of her age hiding in their bedrooms. Not Belinda; she couldn't care less.

'At least now I know how to get Belinda to turn up to meetings on time,' Holly said. 'Hold them here.'

Tracy lifted her sports bag off the spare seat so that Holly could sit down. 'Maybe we should change it from the Mystery Club to the Ice-Cream Club,' she grinned. 'We've certainly had more ice-creams than mysteries lately.'

'That's because nothing mysterious happens round here any more,' said Belinda.

'Oh, I don't know,' said Holly, almost forgetting herself for a moment.

Tracy and Belinda looked at Holly expectantly. 'What's happened?' they said together.

Holly tried to look innocent. 'Nothing,' she said. She really had to keep quiet about the phone call.

6

'Is there something we don't know?' asked Tracy.

Holly shook her head. 'It's Belinda who's got the secret.'

'Me?'

'Didn't you say you had something to tell me? Sounded like it was important.'

Belinda looked blank for a moment then her eyes lit up. 'It is,' she agreed, 'very important.'

'What is it then?'

'Passion fruit and guava tastes even better with chocolate-fudge ripple than apricot and kumquat does.'

Tracy sighed and stood up. 'This girl puts more effort into discovering the perfect combination of ice-cream than Einstein put into discovering the theory of relativity.'

'In Einstein's day they had nothing to choose from – they only had vanilla,' said Belinda. 'Now, if you're going to the counter get me a scoop of rum and raisin.'

To the members of the Mystery Club ice-cream was a serious business. It required total concentration, so for a while no one spoke.

It was Belinda who finally broke the silence. 'Perfect!' she sighed, laying down her spoon. 'The perfect start to a holiday. A full morning's riding followed by five scoops of heaven.'

'How is Meltdown?' asked Tracy. 'Still sagging in the middle?'

Belinda looked outraged. She could stand rude comments about her weight but nobody insulted her beloved horse. 'Meltdown could carry somebody three times my weight without any problem!'

'He may have to,' said Tracy. 'If you keep eating like this, you'll be three times your weight by the end of the holiday!'

'I've never noticed *you* refusing second helpings,' said Belinda.

'No,' agreed Tracy. 'But the difference is I'll be working the weight off at Paradise.'

'Is that where you've been this morning?' asked Holly.

'Yes,' Tracy grinned. 'It's fantastic!'

Paradise was a new health and fitness club that had just opened at Willingston, a small village just outside Willow Dale. As part of its publicity drive it had run a competition in the local paper. The prize was one month's free membership. To Tracy's delight she had won the competition and had chosen to take the prize during the school holidays.

'They've got everything there,' Tracy said. 'Swimming pool, weights room, squash and tennis courts, even a sauna.'

'Well, it's pretty obvious what you're going to be doing this holiday then,' said Holly.

8

'That's right,' said Tracy. 'I'm going to make the most of my month. I'll never be able to afford it after that. It's incredibly expensive. I'm planning to go there every day. By the end of this holiday I'll be so fit you won't recognise me.'

'Yes, we will,' said Belinda. 'You'll be the one with a sports bag in one hand and a triple scoop ice-cream in the other.'

'Better than having a triple scoop ice-cream in one hand and a double scoop in the other,' Tracy laughed. 'What about you, Holly? What are you up to?'

'Well,' said Holly, 'I started off this morning by trying to rearrange my books but then—' Holly paused.

'Then what?'

'Oh, I just had to do something for my mother,' Holly ended lamely.

'You had a phone call,' asked Tracy.

'A phone call?' Suddenly Holly's suspicions flooded back. Her eyes searched Tracy's face for some kind of clue. Was she teasing her? Did she know about the phone call because she'd made it? 'What do you know about a phone call?'

Tracy shrugged. 'Nothing. I just figured that if you suddenly had to do something for your mom, she must have phoned you up from work. Or is she on holiday too?'

9

Holly relaxed a little. 'No, she's not on holiday. I did have a phone call,' Holly agreed.

'Well, at least we sorted *that* out,' Belinda said, winking at Tracy. 'I was beginning to think something strange was going on. Now I'm getting my appetite back. So – who's for seconds?'

'We're for seconds and you're for fourths,' said Tracy.

'I wonder what mint chocolate chip and toffee almond delight are like together?' Belinda said as she headed back to the counter.

Tracy and Belinda waved goodbye as they turned down the alley which led to the bus stop. Holly had pretended that she was going to the library but instead she set off down Market Street towards the Queen's Head Hotel.

The Queen's Head was right in the middle of the old part of Willow Dale. Holly had passed it dozens of times but had never been inside. All she knew was that it was very old and very expensive. There were newer, more up-to-date hotels on the outskirts of Willow Dale. They were more luxurious and had better facilities. But the Queen's Head had history and character, and tourists loved it.

Holly stopped and glanced round the street to make sure no one was watching before stepping inside. Willow Dale wasn't a large town but already Holly knew a lot of people, even though it only seemed like yesterday that the Adams family had moved there from London.

To the left of the reception desk was a lounge. Holly headed straight for a red velvet armchair in the corner. From there she would have a good view of both the front entrance and the staircase to the upper rooms.

As she turned and sat down Holly half expected Tracy and Belinda to come grinning their way towards her. But to her relief there was no sign of them at all.

Holly felt a buzz of excitement deep inside. Suddenly she was sure that this wasn't a joke. She really was going to meet her favourite author! But how would they recognise each other? P.J. Benson had no idea what Holly looked like. And Holly only had the picture on the back of the book to go by. *That'll have to do,* she thought. *I just hope she hasn't changed much.*

The hotel was pretty quiet. Three people were sitting in the lounge and two more were talking to the reception clerk. None of them looked anything like the photograph of P.J. Benson.

Holly checked her watch. It was still only five minutes to four. She sat back and waited.

Just after four o'clock a girl of about fifteen – the same age as Holly – came downstairs and sat nearby. Holly smiled at her but the girl just picked up a magazine and started to flick through it.

By quarter past four there was still no sign of the writer and Holly was beginning to think it might be a hoax after all. Not only that, but the reception clerk kept looking across at her. Holly grabbed a magazine from a nearby table and buried her head in it. The last thing she wanted was to draw attention to herself.

Suddenly a shadow was cast across her and a voice said, 'Excuse me, miss.'

At last! thought Holly. She looked up expecting to see the kindly smile from the back cover of P.J. Benson's latest book. Instead she saw the young, curious face of a waitress. 'Is there anything I can get you?' the girl continued.

'No. No, thank you,' Holly said.

The waitress turned towards the reception clerk and shook her head. He shrugged and looked away. Holly felt her cheeks flush red. She was being made to look stupid. This must all be a practical joke!

At half past four an elderly woman entered from the street. She seemed to be looking for someone. Holly stared at her. She was older than the photograph and her hair was shorter and bleached blonde. But it could just possibly be the author.

Holly put down the magazine but before she could get to her feet, the girl seated nearby rushed across the room and threw her arms round the old woman. A few moments later the two were

12

leaving the hotel arm in arm. Holly was left staring hopelessly after them.

Holly decided she'd waited long enough. She jumped to her feet and strode angrily towards the entrance. A couple of middle-aged American tourists were entering as she reached the door and Holly was forced to stand to one side. They were in the middle of an argument and never even noticed Holly. The door swung shut behind them.

Holly reached out to pull it open but as she did so a hand gripped her arm. Taken by surprise she turned to find herself looking into the face of a woman in her mid-forties. She had short dark hair and the most amazing emerald green eyes.

'What are you doing here?' the woman said in a low voice as though she was anxious no one else should hear.

Holly tried to shake her arm free of the steely grip. 'You're hurting me,' she said. 'Will you let go please?'

The woman repeated the question. 'What are you doing here?'

'What's it got to do with you?'

'Are you Holly Adams?'

Holly stopped struggling.

'Are you?'

Holly nodded.

'Good,' the woman smiled. 'My name is Benson. P.J. Benson.'

Holly shook her head. 'No, you're not,' she said. 'You're nothing like P.J. Benson. I've seen her picture on the back of her books. And you look absolutely nothing like her.'

The woman looked round nervously. 'Don't make a scene, please.'

'Then let go of my arm,' said Holly. 'I don't know what you're up to or who you are or but—'

'No,' the woman interrupted. 'But I know who you are. You're Holly Adams. Your family moved up here a few months ago from London. You go to the Winifred Bowen-Davies School where you've set up something called the Mystery Club with your two friends Tracy and Belinda. And when you wrote to me telling me all that and asking for an interview for your school magazine, you called yourself my number one fan.' The woman smiled again. 'Now how would I know that if I wasn't P.J. Benson?'

Holly's mind raced. 'I've no idea,' she said. 'I just know you look different.'

'I can explain,' the woman said. 'There is a reason. Just trust me. Please.'

Holly stared at her. The woman certainly appeared to be telling the truth. Holly nodded. 'All right then.'

'Excuse me.' The reception clerk was standing behind them. He looked puzzled and embarrassed. 'Sorry to bother you, Mrs Payton,' he said. 'But is there anything wrong?'

14

'Payton?' Holly echoed.

The woman ignored her. 'No, nothing wrong,' she said. 'This is my niece. We arranged to meet here but there was a mix-up over the time. I just managed to catch her as she was leaving.'

The clerk smiled with relief. 'Oh, good,' he said. 'I thought I'd just check.'

Holly was totally bewildered. She watched the clerk return to the reception desk then she turned back to the woman claiming to be P.J. Benson. 'Mrs Payton!' she said.

'I know it must seem strange,' the woman replied. 'But I really can explain. If you'll only give me a chance. Now please come with me. I've got a room booked. We can talk there.'

'No way,' said Holly. 'If you want to explain you can explain down here. And I can tell you now – the explanation had better be good.'

2 The missing photograph

'Would you like coffee or something?'

Holly shook her head.

The woman had led the way to a table in the lounge.

'Are you sure?'

'All I want is an explanation,' Holly insisted. 'If you don't mind.'

The woman nodded understandingly. 'I'm sorry if I alarmed you. It really is very straightforward, though I can't blame you for being suspicious.'

Her eyes scanned Holly's face, searching for some response.

Holly sensed that the woman was trying to win her confidence. But she was determined not to give anything away.

'Are you sure you wouldn't like coffee? Or a soft drink perhaps?' There was a hint of desperation in the woman's voice.

Holly looked at her watch. 'I don't really have that much time,' she said. 'I should be getting home.'

'Of course,' the woman replied. 'It's just that I'm

not very good at this. Meeting new people. I spend a lot of time alone. It's one of the problems of being a writer.'

Holly said nothing.

The woman took a deep breath. 'So what would you like to know?'

'Who are you?'

'P.J. Benson.'

'Then why did the receptionist call you Mrs Payton?'

'I booked in under a false name. I often do it. It's less embarrassing that way. I don't like people knowing I'm an author.'

'I see.' Holly prepared to serve her ace. 'And I suppose you've had plastic surgery as well. To stop you looking like the photograph on the back of your books?'

The woman glanced anxiously over her shoulder. 'I'd really be very grateful if you would keep your voice down,' she said quietly.

'And I'd be grateful if you would just tell me the truth,' Holly snapped.

For a moment the woman was taken aback by Holly's outburst. Then suddenly her face relaxed into a smile. 'You know, Holly,' she said. 'I can see how you've survived all those Mystery Club adventures now. You really can look after yourself, can't you?'

For the first time, Holly began to warm towards

the woman. 'I'm sorry. I didn't mean to be rude,' she said.

The woman waved the apology away. 'You're right to be suspicious. I'm a stranger. You don't know me from Adam. Or should I say Eve?'

Holly smiled.

'You've got to be sure I am who I say I am.'

'I'm glad you understand,' said Holly.

'I do,' the woman continued. 'I know it must all seem very strange to you but like most things in life there's really a very simple explanation. You see, although I always wanted to be a successful writer, I never wanted to be famous. Not recognised in the street. Pointed at. Asked for my autograph. That sort of thing. I'm really a very private person. I like to keep myself to myself. Do you understand?'

Holly thought for a moment. 'Not really,' she said. Holly thought it would be fantastic to be a famous author. Or better still, a famous journalist.

'Not many people do,' the woman sighed, 'Especially publishers. Anyway, when I had my first book published, I told my agent I didn't want any publicity. No photographs. No personal appearances. Nothing. At first that was OK. But once it became a bestseller, people began to get curious. They had all sorts of theories about why I was so secretive. There were even rumours that I was really a man. It built up into quite a mystery actually. So to try and stop all the questions

I gave them a photograph to put on the back cover.'

'But it doesn't look anything like you,' Holly protested.

'That's because it wasn't me. It was a picture of my mother's sister, my Aunty Hilda. We've stuck with that ever since.'

'But it wasn't on your first book?'

'No.'

Holly pushed her chair back from the table and stood up. 'I think I've heard enough,' she said.

The woman was puzzled. 'What's wrong?'

'It's a good story,' Holly said. 'A very good story. But there's one problem with it.'

The woman frowned. 'I don't understand. What problem?'

'I've got a copy of your first book. The one you say was published without a photograph. And I can tell you it's got the same picture on the back as all the others. So what you've just told me is a lie.'

There was a silence. The woman stared up at Holly. There was an amused look in her eyes as she finally spoke. 'You know, Holly, you really do have the makings of a very good detective. All you've got to do is learn to think twice before you speak. You've obviously got a later edition of my first book. When the publishers reprinted it, they added the picture on the back cover.'

Holly sank slowly back into her chair.

19

'The first editions are pretty rare now,' the woman continued. 'But I think I may be able to lay my hands on one. I'll let you have it some day if you're interested.'

Holly felt herself blush a deep shade of pink. How could she have been so stupid? It was an obvious answer. She had thought she was being so clever and all she had done was make herself look foolish.

I – I don't know what to say,' she stammered.

'Please don't apologise. There's nothing wrong with a vivid imagination. It's just that in real life it's usually best to look for more straightforward explanations first. Don't see mysteries where they don't exist.'

Holly opened her mouth to speak but the woman continued, 'And if you want to know why I waited until you were leaving the hotel before I grabbed you, I had no choice. There was another girl waiting. About the same age as you. You must have noticed her. It was only when she left with someone else that I could be certain you were the one I was looking for.'

Holly stared glumly down at the table. 'I am sorry, Miss Benson. It's all so obvious. Why didn't I see it?'

The woman reached over and took her hand. 'You were looking for a more exciting explanation, that's all,' she said kindly. 'And incidentally, friends just call me Benson. Not Miss Benson. It sounds a bit strange at first, I know. But you'll soon get used to it.'

'OK . . . Benson,' Holly grinned.

'That's better,' Benson replied. 'Now maybe we can have that coffee I mentioned earlier.'

By the time the coffee arrived the two were chatting like old friends. Benson told Holly how she'd first had the idea for her cello-playing amateur detective, Penelope Shepherd. And how a meeting with a man on a train had led to the invention of Greville MacWhinney, the bad-tempered, highly eccentric private eye. Holly was fascinated.

Gradually though Benson switched the conversation round to Holly. 'Now what about this Mystery Club,' she asked when Holly had finished talking about her parents and her brother Jamie. 'It sounds like quite something.'

'It is!' Holly agreed. 'It's the best thing I've ever done. I started it soon after I moved here from London. I really missed Miranda and Peter my friends in London. We used to have lots of adventures together. So I thought forming a mystery club would be a good way of making new friends.'

'And was it?' Benson asked.

'You bet it was. Tracy and Belinda are the two best friends anybody could have!'

'And you all love mystery novels?'

'Mysteries – full stop. Especially real-life mysteries.'

'Yes,' Benson laughed. 'You mentioned a couple of your adventures in your letter. You seem to attract them, don't you?'

'There have been others since then,' said Holly. 'If you're interested.'

'I'd love to hear about them.' Benson looked at her watch and stood up. 'But I'm afraid it'll have to be some other time. I've got another appointment in a few minutes. It's an interview.'

Holly frowned. 'I thought—' she started but the writer was ahead of her.

'I know,' she said. 'You thought I didn't do interviews. And I don't – at least, I didn't. Not until now. I've agreed to do one interview with a radio reporter.' Benson was clearly not happy about it. 'It's a kind of compromise with my publishers. They wanted me to do something for newspapers and TV but that would have meant pictures. And pictures are out for obvious reasons. Anyway this radio reporter contacted my publishers and said he'd interview me, then make the interview available to all the local stations. Well, I thought I'd better do it.'

Holly tried not to let her disappointment show. 'I'd better let you go then,' she said.

But Benson didn't move. Instead she said, 'I've just had an idea. Why don't you come and sit in on the interview? You might find it interesting.'

Holly was uncertain. She would love to see how a radio journalist worked. But she didn't want to get in the way.

'It's all right,' said Benson. 'You won't be in the way.' It was almost as though she could read Holly's mind. 'And it's only upstairs.'

'Upstairs?'

'As I explained before, I've taken a room for the afternoon. I don't want any reporter knowing where I live.'

Holly looked at her watch. It was getting late. Her heart sank. 'I wish I could,' she said. 'But I don't want to miss the bus.'

'That's no problem,' the writer said. 'My car's outside. I'll give you a lift home.'

'In that case,' said Holly, 'I'd love to come!'

3 Strange behaviour

'You'll have to excuse me for a moment,' said Benson as she disappeared into the bathroom. She was carrying a small overnight bag. 'I've just got to carry out a few running repairs. Make yourself at home.'

Holly glanced around. She was having difficulty taking it all in. Here she was in a hotel room with her favourite author, who was treating her like a long-lost friend. Tracy and Belinda would never believe it!'

Holly sat on the edge of the bed. Next to it was a small cabinet. And on top of that was a copy of P.J. Benson's latest book. She picked it up and leafed through it.

On the title page someone had scrawled a message in thick black felt-tip pen. It said, 'To Ainsley James, with best wishes from P.J. Benson.' The surname had originally been written as 'Jones' and had been changed to 'James' afterwards.

It seemed that whoever Ainsley James was, Benson didn't know him very well. And she wasn't much bothered about trying to create a good impression with him either, or she would have taken more care with the inscription.

Holly replaced the book carefully in the same position. She blushed again as she thought of how silly she'd been jumping to all the wrong conclusions about P.J. Benson. It was a wonder the writer hadn't sent her packing straight away. That was a lesson she'd just have to learn – not to see mysteries where mysteries didn't exist.

A knock on the door jolted Holly back to the present.

'Holly! Would you get that please?' Benson called from the bathroom.

Holly jumped up and opened the door. A tall man wearing a dark blue raincoat smiled broadly at Holly. 'Now it's only a guess,' he said, 'but somehow I don't think you are P.J. Benson.'

'No,' Holly replied. 'But this is P.J. Benson's room.'

'Pure luck,' the man laughed. 'I'm the world's worst at finding my way around. Usually it takes me at least three goes before I get the right place. I'm Ainsley James, by the way, I've come to interview the famous mystery writer. May I come in?'

'Yes, of course,' Holly stood back from the doorway and Ainsley James stepped in. He had dark curly hair and deep brown eyes. But the most noticeable thing about him was the wonderful smile. It was one of those smiles that made you feel that there was no one else he would rather be with. It was magnetic and Holly couldn't take her eyes off him.

'Is something wrong?' he said, unbuttoning his raincoat.

Holly felt herself blushing again. 'No,' she said. 'Sorry, I was just thinking of something else.'

'I'm not the world's most fascinating person,' he joked. 'But usually I manage to keep people's attention for more than fifteen seconds.'

'I'm sorry,' Holly repeated. 'Benson – I mean, Miss Benson, will be with you in a minute.'

'That's fine,' James replied. 'It'll give me time to get my trusty machine ready.' He was already undoing the press-studs of a black leather case that had been slung over his shoulder. 'And time to get to know you, of course.'

He turned the smile on Holly again. In spite of her embarrassment she couldn't look away. She was transfixed like a rabbit caught in a car's headlights.

'That was a hint actually,' he said. 'I was hoping you might tell me your name.'

'Sorry,' Holly apologised again. 'It's Holly. Holly Adams.'

Over the next few minutes, Ainsley James effortlessly went through the preparations for his interview. Chairs placed in position. Microphone plugged in. New tape wound on, batteries checked. And as he worked he asked Holly an endless stream of questions. But in such an easy way that it seemed the most natural conversation in the world.

By the time everything was set up, Holly had told the reporter about her family's move from London, her mother's job at the bank, her father's new career making furniture and her brother's total obsession with computer games. She was about to start on the Mystery Club when the bathroom door opened and P.J. Benson stepped out.

For a moment Holly was stunned by what she saw. The writer had completely changed her appearance! She had added twenty years to her age. A silver-grey wig hid her short dark hair and a pair of round, horn-rimmed glasses seemed to change the shape of her face entirely. It wasn't the face of the woman on the book covers but it was close enough to make someone think that it might be.

Benson immediately took control of the situation. 'You must be Mr James,' she said, offering her hand. 'I'm so sorry to have kept you waiting.'

Ainsley James hesitated for just one moment and then shook hands. 'Wonderful to meet you,' he said. 'I'm a great fan of yours. A great fan.'

'Thank you. You understand that I'm not prepared to answer anything at all about my private life, don't you?'

The reporter's smile was working overtime. 'I understand perfectly,' he said. 'And I don't blame you for one moment. There are things in most people's lives that they prefer to keep quiet about. Skeletons in the cupboard. Secrets that could cause a lot of trouble if they ever got out. Not that I'm suggesting there are any skeletons in your cupboard, of course.'

Benson seemed uncertain how to react. 'I'm glad to hear it,' she replied at last. 'Now perhaps we could get on. I don't have too much time.'

The reporter nodded understandingly. 'Of course. If you'll just sit right here we can get underway.' He ushered Benson into a chair and then turned his attention to Holly. 'Perhaps you'd like to pop downstairs and grab a coffee while we do this?' he said to her. 'It'll only take about twenty minutes.'

Holly was caught out by the suggestion. She looked to Benson for help.

'I'd like Holly to sit in on the interview,' the writer insisted. 'She wants to be a journalist. She thinks she might learn something.'

For a moment the reporter's smile flickered uneasily. 'I doubt whether she'll learn much from watching me,' he said. The smile returned full beam. 'But of course, you're welcome to see. After all, I've got nothing to hide.'

The reporter sat on the chair next to Benson. He lifted the microphone and switched on the tape machine.

Even to a beginner like Holly it was obvious that Ainsley James was good at his job. Each question flowed easily and naturally from the previous one and he seemed to be genuinely interested in the answers. He also had the ability to put the other person at ease so that by the end of the interview P.J. Benson seemed to be enjoying talking about her work.

'That was fascinating,' the reporter said as he packed away the recorder. 'Absolutely fascinating. I hope it wasn't too painful for you.'

'Surprisingly enough it wasn't,' Benson replied. She looked across at Holly. 'I wonder if you would just pass me that book on the bedside cabinet, please, Holly?'

Holly picked up the book and handed it across the bed.

'I really did find it very interesting,' Ainsley James said, as he swung the recorder over his shoulder. 'Not that I should find that surprising. I was told you were a very good speaker.'

Benson, who had been checking the inscription at the front of the book, suddenly looked up. 'Told?' she repeated. 'Who told you that?'

'Someone I interviewed a few months ago,' Ainsley James replied. 'A woman called McLean. Janice McLean, I think her name was. She said she'd met you a few years back.'

Benson suddenly turned and walked across to the dressing-table. She had her back towards Holly and the reporter but from where Holly sat she could see the writer's face in the mirror. She looked strained and nervous.

'I think you must be mistaken,' she said quietly. 'I've never met anyone by that name.'

'Really?' the reporter seemed surprised by Benson's response. 'Maybe I've got the name wrong. I really am terrible with names. I think she said she was a friend of your brother. You do have a brother, don't you? Or have I got it all wrong?'

There was an awkward pause. Benson seemed to be lost in thought.

The reporter broke the silence. 'I'm sorry, that's a personal question, isn't it? And we agreed no personal questions.' He turned to Holly. 'You see, Holly,' he smiled, 'you have learned something from me after all. Even if only how not to do it.' He held out his hand. 'Time I was going anyway. I'll let you good people get on with your lives.'

Holly shook hands.

The reporter turned his attention back to the writer. 'Unless, of course, you'd like to carry on our conversation down in the bar? I'm sure there are lots of things we could talk about.'

'I'm afraid that won't be possible,' Benson replied. 'I've got too much to do.'

'Well, I'll tell you what. I'll be down there for the next half an hour or so, if you should change your mind,' said Ainsley James.

Benson turned briefly to face him. Her smile was tight and unconvincing. 'I'll think about it,' she said.

The reporter's smile broadened. 'Wonderful!' he beamed. 'Goodbye then, Holly. And good luck with the reporting!'

The moment the door closed behind the reporter, Benson rapidly began collecting together her belongings. The book which she had inscribed to Ainsley James was now on the dressing-table.

Holly hurried over and picked it up. 'Benson,' she said, 'you forgot the book. Shall I run after Mr James and give it to him?'

'What?' Benson seemed surprised to find Holly still in the room.

'This book. You were going to give it to Mr James.'

'Don't be silly,' Benson grabbed the book out of Holly's hands. 'I had no intention of giving the book to him. What made you think that?'

All the friendliness had disappeared from the writer's manner. For a moment she stared angrily at Holly. Then her eyes softened slightly. 'I'm really

31

very sorry,' she said. 'But I have to get away. It's been nice meeting you.' Benson disappeared into the bathroom, leaving Holly staring after her.

Holly was confused. It seemed that she had said or done something to upset the writer. But she couldn't work out what it was.

When Benson emerged from the bathroom she had removed the disguise and was carrying the overnight bag. Quickly she checked round the room. Satisfied she was leaving nothing behind, she headed for the door.

Holly cleared her throat nervously.

Benson stopped. 'Is something wrong?'

'No. It's just . . . well, you said you'd give me a lift back.'

'A lift?'

Holly nodded. 'Or are you staying to speak to Mr James?'

'Oh, no. Definitely not. After all, I did promise to give you a lift and I couldn't break my promise.'

'Are you sure?'

'Yes. But you'll have to hurry. I'm in a rush.'

The writer was already moving towards the door. Out in the corridor, she turned away from the main stairs and headed instead towards the fire exit. 'We'll go this way,' she said. 'It's quicker. And I've already paid the bill.'

The fire exit led down the outside of the building into a small carpark at the rear of the hotel.

In the corner of the carpark was a silver-grey Toyota.

Benson deactivated the car alarm. 'Get in,' she told Holly.

Holly was still putting on the seat belt as Benson accelerated at speed across the carpark.

The traffic in front of the Queen's Head Hotel was one way. Benson turned into the stream of cars without stopping. A white van braked heavily and beeped its horn but the writer seemed not to hear it.

Holly began to wonder if she wouldn't have been better off waiting for the later bus.

Benson was adjusting her driving mirror, looking for traffic behind. Holly glanced over her shoulder. A dark-coloured saloon was moving up quickly behind them.

'It's best to turn left at the end here,' Holly said.

Benson began to indicate. She checked her mirror. The car behind was also indicating left. Benson approached the T-junction in the left-hand lane. But at the last moment she veered across the road and turned right, narrowly missing a traffic bollard.

There was a screeching of brakes as the car behind skidded to a stop.

'Sorry,' said Benson almost immediately. 'Somehow I'd got it in my head that it was this way.' The writer was staring into her rear-view mirror again.

'It's OK though,' she said. 'I'm sure you must know a different route.'

At the next set of traffic-lights Benson accelerated hard as the lights changed to amber. Again she stared into her rear-view mirror. Holly looked behind. There were no other cars in sight.

For the first time since leaving the hotel P.J. Benson seemed to relax a little. 'Sorry,' she said to Holly. 'I hate driving in heavy traffic. Now, which way do I go?'

Benson pulled the car smoothly into the side of the road. 'Are you sure you don't want me to take you right to the door?' she asked Holly. 'It's no problem.'

'No, thanks,' Holly said as she got out. 'It's easier for you if you stay on the main road. Where do you have to go now?'

Benson was already indicating to pull out. 'I'll find my way,' she said.

Holly felt uncomfortable at the writer's impatience to get away but she knew what she had to ask. She wasn't going to let a chance like this just disappear.

'I don't want to be a nuisance,' Holly said. 'But you did say you might be willing to do an interview for the school magazine.'

'Perhaps,' said Benson, checking over her shoulder. 'I haven't decided yet.'

'But I don't know how to get in touch with you.'

'You won't need to,' Benson said. 'If I decide to do it, I'll contact you.'

Holly closed the door and the silver-grey saloon sped off.

4   False identity

Tracy took three steps forward and dived into the pool. The water closed over her head. The next moment she broke the surface in a mass of bubbles. Lazily, she slipped into an effortless breaststroke and glided towards the centre of the pool.

At the far end, a lone swimmer was ploughing backwards and forwards across the width. He was swimming head down in a clumsy front crawl that succeeded in splashing water everywhere but hardly moved him forward at all. He reminded Tracy of a water buffalo!

The pool at Paradise was much smaller than the one at the Willow Dale Leisure Centre. A width would not take a serious swimmer more than half a dozen strokes.

Gently Tracy eased her way down the length. The Water Buffalo was crossing and recrossing her path in a flurry of flailing arms and legs.

He probably doesn't even realise I'm here, Tracy thought as the man splashed past not more than a metre in front of her.

36

The instant his feet were clear she swept forward. Three strokes later her hands were gripping the end rail. Looking across she saw that the other swimmer had also stopped. Grabbing the opportunity she turned and pushed away from the side. At the same moment, the man hurled himself backwards.

His head thudded against Tracy's hip, then disappeared beneath the surface. Desperately clutching out to save himself, his hands fastened on Tracy's leg, taking her down with him.

As her head sank beneath the water, Tracy kicked out to break the man's grip then twisted back towards the surface. Grasping the side rail with one hand, she reached down into the water with the other. Her fingers closed on the man's wrist. Using all her strength she heaved him to the side.

As his head emerged, Tracy realised she had seen the man before. The previous day he had created a terrible scene in the sun lounge after a waitress had brought him grapefruit juice when he claimed to have ordered orange juice. The waitress took the blame. But both she and Tracy, who was sitting nearby, knew that the man had definitely asked for grapefruit.

At first, the man was too busy coughing and spluttering to take notice of Tracy. When he did finally look across at her, his eyes narrowed and his mouth twisted into a snarl. 'What do you think you're up to?' he snapped. 'You could've drowned me, you idiot!'

Tracy was so surprised she didn't know to say. She hadn't expected a medal, just a simple word of thanks. She got neither.

'What are you? Stupid or blind?' the man carried on. 'Couldn't you see me? I mean, the pool's not exactly crowded, is it? Or perhaps you did it deliberately?'

'I didn't do anything. Apart from pull you out!' Tracy exclaimed. 'You threw yourself backwards on top of me. You never even looked to see if there was anybody behind you.'

'Oh, I see; it's my fault is it? You half drown me and it's my fault. You kids! You're all the same. Nothing but trouble. I don't know why they allow you in here.'

Before Tracy could reply, the bad-tempered man was clambering up on to the side. As his legs came out of the pool he kicked out and sent a spray of water into Tracy's face.

By the time Tracy had cleared the water from her eyes, he had grabbed his towel and bathrobe and was stalking off towards the changing-rooms.

Tracy immediately threw herself into a fast front crawl, taking all her fury out on the water. It had been a long time since she had felt so angry with anyone.

After a dozen lengths of hard swimming her

temper had cooled. She pulled herself out on to the side and noticed something glinting in the sunlight. She bent down and picked it up. It was a gold watch.

It wasn't new but it did look very expensive. Tracy turned it over in her hand. The back of the watch was hallmarked and engraved with the owner's initials.

It must belong to the Water Buffalo, Tracy said to herself. It had probably dropped out of the pocket of his bathrobe.

Tracy toyed with the idea of throwing it into the pool but her conscience got the better of her. She wouldn't sink to his level, she thought. She'd hand it in at reception on her way home.

Steve Biggins was looking after the reception desk. He was a sixth former at the Winifred Bowen-Davies School and was hoping to do a degree in Sport and Leisure. So he was working at Paradise over the holidays to gain experience.

'I found this by the side of the swimming pool,' Tracy told him. 'I think it must belong to the man who was swimming in there earlier. Middle-aged, heavy, thick-set and bald on top with short black hair round the sides and back.'

'You mean Mr Crawford,' Steve said instantly.

'Crawford?' Tracy repeated.

'Yes. Peter Crawford.'

'I don't think so,' Tracy said.

'Definitely,' Steve insisted. 'He's the only person staying here that looks anything like that. Usually he wears tinted glasses. But I suppose he leaves those off when he's swimming.'

Tracy thought back to the previous day. The man in the sun lounge had been wearing tinted glasses.

'Yes,' she agreed. 'I guess that's him all right. Peter Crawford, you say his name is?'

'That's right. I'll pass this on to him. Looks expensive. Maybe you'll get a reward.'

'I doubt it,' said Tracy.

'So do I,' said Steve, dropping his voice. 'He's more likely to report you for theft.'

'You don't like him?'

'Like him? I don't know what it is with him, but he's been nothing but trouble ever since he arrived.'

'Thanks,' said Tracy as she walked towards the door. 'That's just what I thought.'

'I've always thought that mystery writers must be weird,' said Belinda. 'Otherwise they wouldn't think up such strange stories.'

Holly, Tracy and Belinda were sitting in Holly's bedroom. Holly had given a lot of thought to what had happened at the hotel. Finally, she had decided to call a meeting of the Mystery Club to discuss it.

40

'Even so,' said Holly, 'there must be some explanation for it all.'

Tracy was looking at the photograph on the back of P.J. Benson's latest book. 'And you say she didn't look anything like this,' she said.

'Not even vaguely.'

'Then maybe it wasn't her, after all.'

'If it wasn't her, how could she know all the details of my letter?'

'OK! So it *was* her and she just wants to avoid publicity. Like she said.'

'If I were famous I'd want everyone to know,' said Belinda, grabbing the book from Tracy.

'I don't know,' said Tracy. 'When my picture was in the paper for winning the health club competition it was annoying having people stop me around school and in the street.'

'I won't get tired of being recognised when I win a gold medal in the Olympics Five Day Event,' sighed Belinda.

'The only medal you're likely to get is for the five-bowl event in the Ice-Cream Olympics,' Tracy laughed.

'Yeah,' Belinda agreed. 'A bronze medal. With you two getting the gold and silver ahead of me.'

Holly hurled a pillow at Belinda. 'Let's get back to the mystery,' she said.

But Tracy wasn't sure there was a mystery. 'What else is there?' she said.

'There's the disguise for a start. Then the way she suddenly changed. One minute she was really friendly, the next she couldn't get rid of me fast enough.'

'That I can understand,' joked Belinda.

'And she drove like a maniac. As though she was being followed. And all because that reporter said he'd met somebody who knew her brother.'

'Maybe she doesn't like her brother,' Belinda suggested. 'That's not all that unusual, is it?' she added, looking meaningfully at Holly.

'Never mind about the brother. Tell us about the reporter,' said Tracy. 'He sounds cute.'

'Here I am trying to solve a mystery and all you can do is drool over some radio journalist,' Holly protested. 'Isn't anybody going to help?'

Belinda jumped up off her chair. 'Yes,' she shouted excitedly. 'I've found it! The answer was here in the book all the time. Listen!' Belinda opened the back cover of the book and pretended to read out loud. '"About the author: P.J. Benson is a secrecy freak who goes to any lengths to avoid publicity. She even puts somebody else's picture on the back of her books. She frequently phones up total strangers and arranges to meet them in hotel lobbies. After giving them a fright, she pretends to be best buddies and then starts acting weird. P.J. Benson does not appear in her own books because nobody would believe

42

in her."' She shut the book. 'See – all perfectly straightforward.'

Holly took the book off her. 'Very funny,' she said placing the book back on the shelf. 'Anyway, I reckon I've seen the last of P.J. Benson. Which is a pity. Getting that interview would have been a real scoop.'

'Talking about scoops,' Belinda began.

'Oh, no, she's starting on ice-cream again,' Tracy interrupted.

Belinda perched on the edge of the bed with her back to Tracy. 'Ignore her,' she said. 'She's got an ice-cream fixation. Comes from having too much of it as a child. The scoop I'm talking about is a real hot story for the school magazine.'

Suddenly Holly was interested. 'A story? What is it?'

'It's about a horse!'

Holly and Tracy moaned and held their heads.

'No, really,' Belinda insisted. 'It's a great story. Have you ever heard of the "Blushing Bride"?'

'I thought it was about a horse, not a wedding.'

'Shut up, Tracy. It is about a horse – the Blushing Bride is a horse. One of the best in Britain. And it's being stabled at Hanover Hall.'

Hanover Hall was a large Victorian country house set in its own grounds about eight kilometres outside Willow Dale.

'Hanover Hall?' Holly repeated. 'I thought it was empty.'

'It was. Until this week,' said Belinda. 'They moved in at the weekend. Nobody's supposed to know about it, actually. But I overheard the farrier telling his wife while I was waiting for Meltdown to be shod. He said it was a real rush. They've had people working there all week trying to get the stables ready on time. Quite a story, eh?'

'Belinda, if nobody's supposed to know about it, they're hardly likely to agree to my writing an article for the school magazine, are they?' Holly pointed out.

Belinda looked crestfallen. 'I hadn't thought of that,' she said. 'It's a pity, because if you were doing a story I could come with you. I'd love to get a close look at a horse like that.'

'Another scoop bites the dust,' said Tracy. 'Looks like there's only one big story left. And that's mine.'

Tracy told the tale of the man at the health club: the scene with the waitress, the incident in the swimming pool, and finding the man's watch. At the end she sat back and waited for their reaction.

'He sounds like a nasty piece of work. I'd keep well away from him if I were you,' Belinda warned.

'That's probably good advice,' Holly agreed.

'*What*?' Tracy exploded. 'And miss out on a real-life mystery?'

Holly and Belinda looked at each other. 'A mystery?' they repeated.

'You bet!' said Tracy. 'There's more to Mr Water Buffalo than meets the eye.'

'Explain,' said Holly.

Tracy's eyes lit up. 'It's the watch. That's what gave the game away. See, Steve said his name was Crawford – Peter Crawford. But the initials on the back of his watch were M.J.B. Now I don't know about you, but in my book that is the beginnings of a mystery!'

5 Old friends

Holly was puzzling over the mysteries of P.J. Benson and Peter Crawford long after Tracy and Belinda had gone home. 'Try not to see mysteries where mysteries don't exist.' That was what the writer had said. Yet Holly had a gut feeling that there was more to both situations than met the eye. When she fell asleep she dreamed of a disguised writer, wearing a gold wristwatch, riding a water buffalo the wrong way down a one-way street!

It was almost a quarter to nine when Holly woke the next morning. She pulled on her dressing-gown and hurried downstairs. Her mother was just leaving for the bank.

'I looked in through your door,' she called to Holly from the car. 'But you looked like you'd had a disturbed night.'

'I did,' Holly shouted back. 'One or two things on my mind. I'll tell you about them later.'

Mrs Adams waved and started the car engine. 'Go and see your dad; he's got some great news.'

Holly headed towards the kitchen. She thought

46

she might just catch her father before he disappeared off to his workshop.

At the kitchen table, Jamie was busy working his way through a packet of sugared cornflakes and a pint of milk.

'Hi! Seen Dad?' Holly asked.

Jamie grunted something which could have been 'He's in the workshop', or it might even have been 'Go shove your head in a bucket'. Either way Holly decided to look for herself.

Mr Adams was sanding down a table-top. A fine mist of sawdust hung in the air. Holly waited for her father to switch off the sander before she joined him.

'How long have you been up?' he asked, lifting his goggles and taking off his ear protectors. 'Your mother said you were still asleep.'

'I was,' Holly admitted. 'I caught her as she was going off to work. She said you had some news.'

Mr Adams shook the sawdust out of his hair and grinned. 'I have,' he said. 'Late last night I had a phone call. It was a reporter. Wanting to do an interview with me.'

'An interview? With you?' Holly was puzzled. 'What about?'

Her father waved his hands around. 'About all this,' he said. 'It is a bit unusual, you know. It's not every day that the world's greatest lawyer gives up his high-powered London practice and moves to Yorkshire to become the world's greatest furniture-maker. Why else would a reporter want to talk to me?'

Holly shrugged. 'I thought perhaps he wanted to interview the father of the world's greatest mystery-solver.'

Mr Adams laughed. 'You always have to have the last word, don't you?'

Holly put her arm round his waist and squeezed. 'Sorry, Dad. Only joking,' she said. 'It really is great news. Maybe it will get you a lot of extra orders.'

'I need them. To keep you in mystery books and Jamie in computer games. By the way, are you going out this morning?'

'I hadn't planned to.'

'In that case, listen for the doorbell. When the reporter comes, bring him out here. And for goodness sake, keep Jamie away from him!'

Holly couldn't have been more pleased with her father's news. Publicity was just what he needed. A good article with lots of pictures could bring in orders from all over the country. She began to wonder who the article was for. Perhaps it was one of the big colour supplements. More likely though it was one of the local papers – perhaps the *Willow Dale Express*. Still, every little helped.

At about ten thirty the doorbell rang. Holly hurried downstairs from her bedroom but when she answered it, it was just one of Jamie's friends.

Holly went back upstairs and began leafing through a sheaf of magazines, looking for inspiration. Over the holiday everyone had to complete a project. To nobody's surprise, Belinda was planning something about horses. Tracy had decided on a study entitled 'A Day in the Life of a Health and Fitness Centre'. But Holly was still searching for a subject.

The next time the doorbell rang, Holly was surprised to find that it was very nearly midday. In fact, she had been so engrossed in the magazines that she had almost forgotten her father's interview.

As she opened the front door, Holly half expected to see one of Jamie's friends clutching a joystick and a computer disk. Instead she was greeted by the stunning smile of Ainsley James.

For a few seconds, neither of them spoke. Then the reporter broke the silence. 'Of course,' he said, 'I should have realised. Your name is Adams as well, isn't it?'

Holly nodded. 'But I don't see . . .' Her voice trailed off.

'Don't you remember? It's Ainsley James. We met the other day at the hotel.'

'Of course I remember,' Holly said. 'But what are you doing here?'

Ainsley James frowned. 'I've come here to record an interview,' he said. 'With a Mr Adams. About furniture-making. I have got the right place, haven't I?'

Holly felt the blood rush to her cheeks. 'I'm sorry,' she said. 'For some reason I'd got it in my head that this was a newspaper interview. I never dreamed it would be you.'

'Don't worry,' Ainsley James replied. 'What about me? I hadn't thought that it might be your father – and you had mentioned his new career making furniture. Still I think that makes us just about even in the stupidity stakes, doesn't it?'

Holly stood back and Ainsley James stepped inside.

'I must say this is a pleasant surprise,' he smiled. 'Meeting up again so soon. How are you? And how's Miss Benson? She's not here as well, is she?'

'No,' Holly laughed. 'Unless she's come along with you.'

'Afraid not.' The reporter glanced round as though anxious not to be overheard. 'Just between the two of us,' he whispered, the smile still playing around his lips, 'I think I managed to upset her somehow. She never did come down for that drink, you know.'

Holly decided it was best not to say too much about the events at the hotel. 'Maybe she had to rush off somewhere,' she suggested vaguely.

Even though the reporter was still smiling broadly, his eyes were watching Holly closely. For a moment she felt slightly uneasy with the attention the reporter was paying her.

'I'd better take you through to the workshop,' she said. 'My father's waiting for you.'

'Of course,' James replied. 'By the way, what sort of things does he make? Sofas, armchairs, things like that?'

'That's more upholstery than carpentry,' said Holly as she led the way through to the workshop.

'Of course,' said Ainsley James.

Mr Adams had started to French-polish the table-top. But as soon as Holly entered with Ainsley James, he stopped what he was doing and began wiping his hands.

'No,' said the reporter, walking over to him, 'Don't stop, please. I'd love to watch you in action for a while. I've been looking forward to it all morning. It's fascinating – watching a real craftsman at work.'

Holly could tell by the look on her father's face that Ainsley James had said exactly the right thing. The two men were soon deep in conversation. Holly decided that refreshments would be needed and slipped away to the kitchen.

It really is an amazing coincidence, Holly thought as she spooned coffee into the percolator. *Meeting up again. And so soon after the last time.*

Then she realised. She still hadn't told her parents about the meeting with P.J. Benson. What if Ainsley James mentioned it to her father? How would he react?

The moment he entered the kitchen, Holly was certain that her father knew. He had an exasperated look on his face.

'I hear you already know Mr James,' he said, washing his hands at the kitchen sink.

'I've been meaning to tell you about that,' said Holly.

'You can tell us tonight,' said Mr Adams. 'After dinner. I expect it's a long story and I'm sure your mother won't want to miss it.'

Holly poured out three mugs of coffee and handed one to Ainsley James. 'Me and my big mouth,' he whispered to her.

'I hope I haven't landed you in any trouble,' he said later, as Holly opened the front door to let him out.

Holly smiled. 'It's OK,' she said. 'It was no big secret; I just hadn't got round to telling them yet. And they're quite used to surprises by now.'

'So your father was saying – something about a Mystery Club, isn't it?'

'That's right,' Holly admitted.

'I hope you take care,' said Ainsley James. 'Some mysteries can be very dangerous.'

The reporter stepped out on to the path. 'I imagine that's why you're so friendly with P.J. Benson?' Ainsley James paused for a moment. As though he'd just thought of something. 'I don't suppose you've got an address for her, have you? I wanted to let her have a cassette of the interview.'

Holly shook her head. 'I can't help you. I wish I could.'

'Phone number?'

'Sorry,' said Holly. Then she had a thought. 'Couldn't you contact her through that friend of her brother?'

For a second the reporter looked shocked. Then a broad grin spread across his face. 'That's a very good idea. Why didn't I think of that?' He held out his hand. 'Goodbye,' he said. 'For now.'

The reporter turned and walked towards his small green Citroën. His tape recorder slung over one shoulder.

'I've just thought,' Holly called after him. 'When is Dad's interview going to be broadcast?'

Ainsley James opened the car door. 'I haven't actually sold it to anybody yet,' he said. 'But it shouldn't be difficult. I'll let you know when I do.'

Holly waved as the car pulled away, then hurried back to the workshop.

Mr Adams looked quite pleased with himself. 'He

really is a very good interviewer. I thought I'd be nervous but he put me completely at my ease.'

Holly perched on the edge of the workbench. The reporter certainly had the knack of winning people over. She'd seen him work his magic on two people now, her father and P.J. Benson. Yet right at the end Benson had taken against him. Even the reporter himself had realised it.

Mr Adams had gone back to the table-top, applying the polish in small overlapping circles. Suddenly he stopped and looked up. 'The only thing I find puzzling,' he said, 'is how he found out about me in the first place.'

'Didn't you ask him? What did he say?'

'Something about meeting somebody somewhere who'd bought something I'd made. I never found out who.' Mr Adams went back to his polishing. 'You didn't tell him then?'

'Who didn't?' said a voice from the doorway.

Holly turned round to see her mother standing there.

'What are you doing here?' Mr Adams said. 'I wasn't expecting you back for lunch.'

Mrs Adams carefully picked her way across the workshop and kissed her husband on the cheek. 'I had to find out how you'd got on with the reporter. Unfortunately I'll have to hurry. I'm already late. I got held up along the road. Two cars were parked side by side blocking the way. The drivers seemed to think it was the perfect place to have a chat. A dark blue saloon. And one of those funny French cars.'

Holly's ears pricked up. 'A green one?' she asked.

'I think it might have been. Anyway, it's not important. I didn't come back to talk about inconsiderate drivers. Tell me about the interview instead.'

Holly put down her knife and fork. 'I know I should have told you earlier,' she said. 'It's just that Benson was so definite about me not saying anything.'

Mr and Mrs Adams looked at each other across the remains of the evening meal. They had spent the last half hour listening to every detail of Holly's meeting with P.J. Benson.

'She certainly seems to be a bit of a strange character,' Holly's mother admitted. 'But I can understand her wanting to keep her privacy. If people knew she was around she'd get all sorts of people bothering her. Fans. Weirdos. Reporters.'

'I can vouch for that,' Mr Adams agreed with a grin. 'We famous celebrities are for ever having our work interrupted by reporters. I'm thinking of going into hiding myself.'

'It's gone to his head already,' said Mrs Adams.

'Seriously though. Spending all your time writing mysteries is bound to catch up with you sooner or later,' Mr Adams said. 'She's probably just a bit eccentric.'

'Well, I think it's more than that,' said Holly.

Mrs Adams stood up and began collecting together the dirty plates. 'You know your trouble, Holly?' she sighed as she moved towards the kitchen. 'You're too ready to see mysteries where there are none.'

'Your mother's right, Holly,' said Mr Adams gathering up the glasses. 'You'll see. Next time you meet her she'll probably be perfectly normal.'

Holly pulled a face. 'I've got a feeling there won't be a next time. And that means I've missed out on the biggest interview I've ever had.'

Holly started to fold the tablecloth when the phone in the hall began to ring.

'It's all right,' Mrs Adams shouted from the kitchen. 'I'll get it.'

Holly had just put the tablecloth into the sideboard drawer when her mother came back into the room. 'It's P.J. Benson,' she said to Holly. 'She wants to speak to you.'

6 Over the top

Belinda reined Meltdown back at the brow of the hill and dismounted. The view from the top was amazing. The ground ahead dropped down into a flat-bottomed valley surrounded on three sides by hills. A network of streams tumbled down the slopes and found their way into a river, lazily winding its way across the landscape.

At one point, a sideshoot from the river fed an artificial lake. The lake was overlooked by a large grey-stone building. This was Hanover Hall, the country house where the Blushing Bride was being stabled.

With any luck, Belinda had told herself before she set off, *I'll be able to get a look at her.*

Belinda swung herself back into the saddle. From this point on, the bridle-path curved round to the right. Then it skirted behind a small wood before joining the road that led down towards the Hall.

Meltdown set off along the bridle-path towards the cluster of trees. As the path passed behind the wood, roots from the trees broke the surface, making the ground dangerously uneven. Instinctively Meltdown slowed down.

In one place, the branches of an oak jutted out over the bridle-path. It was then, as she ducked low to avoid them, that Belinda first heard the voices. Men's voices. Coming from inside the wood.

Meltdown bridled slightly at the unexpected noise. Belinda brought him to a halt and listened. For a moment there was silence. Then the voices began again. Belinda thought she heard the words 'It's the best view we can get.' Then a second voice, much closer, added, 'As long as they can't see us.'

Belinda urged Meltdown forward. 'C'mon boy,' she whispered. 'Let's get down on to the road as quickly as possible.' It was a little-used path. No place to meet strangers.

Meltdown picked up speed slightly. But the path was treacherous and he was wary of his footing. Belinda could see the lane ahead now. From the edge of the wood, the bridle-path fell away sharply to get down to the level of the road. They had almost reached this point when without warning a man's figure appeared in front of them.

It was hard to say who was most alarmed; Meltdown shied away and the man threw himself backwards against one of the trees.

'What are you doing?' he cried out. 'Keep that horse away from me.'

'It's all right,' Belinda said. 'He won't hurt you. You just took him by surprise, that's all.'

The man eased away from the tree. He was short and stocky, and wore the kind of outdoor clothing normally found in ex-army surplus stores. His long, grey hair was swept back into a pony-tail. And around his neck hung a pair of high-power binoculars.

'It's a bit dangerous, isn't it?' There was an edge to the man's voice. 'Riding a horse along here?'

'It is a bridle-path,' said Belinda quickly. 'I checked on the map.'

'Maybe it is. But it's a bit lonely. Not the place to have an accident. I'd keep away from here if I were you.'

To Belinda it sounded more like a threat than advice. 'If it's so dangerous,' she demanded, 'what are you doing here?'

'Just passing through.' He tapped the binoculars hanging against his chest. 'Doing a bit of bird-watching.'

Belinda felt uneasy. She twitched the reins. 'I'd best be getting on,' she said. 'Just stand still while we pass and he'll be OK.'

All the time the man had been glancing anxiously towards the road. As Belinda started forward he raised an arm to stop her.

'I was just wondering,' he said hesitantly. Then he stopped as though he was trying to think of something to say. 'Are there any pubs round here?'

Belinda urged Meltdown on. 'Sorry,' she said over her shoulder. 'No idea.'

As they neared the end of the bridle-path, Belinda checked behind. The man was following them down the path.

A few more paces and they turned on to the open road. Belinda breathed a sigh of relief. But another surprise was waiting for her.

A red transit van was pulled over on the verge at the side of the road. The rear doors were open, and a man in a green anorak was unloading something from the back. At the sound of Meltdown's hooves on the tarmac he twisted round. He had short cropped hair and a black moustache.

Belinda kicked Meltdown forward. She had no intention of waiting around. As Meltdown clattered past, Belinda noticed that the man seemed to be unloading a tent from the van. And inside, she caught a glimpse of sleeping bags and a stove. Whoever they were and whatever they were up to, they were planning a long stay.

Belinda didn't stop again until they reached the bridge over the river. From there she looked back up the hill. The wood was clearly visible. So was the red van, still parked at the side of the road. Suddenly something else caught her eye.

A flashing light, like sunlight reflecting on glass.

It was coming from the edge of the wood at the top of the hill. It happened several times in one spot. Then again a short distance away.

What is going on up there? Belinda wondered. *It's a funny place to be camping out. Even for bird-watchers.*

Meltdown stirred impatiently. He was eager to get on. Belinda switched her attention back to the road. There was a stone bridge over the river and then almost immediately a wide tree-lined drive-way which led up to the main part of Hanover Hall. The stables, though, lay alongside the road and were reached by a second entrance about a kilometre further on.

The stable buildings formed a square round a large stable yard, hidden from the road by a high wall. As Belinda rode alongside the wall she thought she could hear the sound of a horse clattering around on the other side. Her hopes rose. Perhaps she would get a good look at the Blushing Bride, after all.

As Belinda and Meltdown neared the entrance to the stables the sound of an approaching engine started to make itself heard. Belinda looked back over her shoulder. A battered-looking farm lorry was thundering down the hill towards the bridge. It was travelling much too fast for the narrow road.

Already Meltdown was getting nervous. Belinda brought the horse to a stop just before the entrance to the stable yard. No matter how close she got to the wall there was going to be a problem. And if anything came along in the opposite direction it would be even worse.

Belinda looked around. There was a large notice by the entrance to the stable yard:

KEEP OUT.
Entry without prior permission strictly prohibited.

Belinda checked behind. Just before the bridge, the road curved sharply to the right so for a moment the lorry was hidden from sight. As she waited for it to come back into view Belinda made a decision.

It can't do any harm, she told herself. *Just popping in there for a couple of minutes.*

She urged Meltdown forward through the entrance and into the stable yard. Almost immediately they found themselves facing another horse. It was being ridden by a girl not much older than Belinda. She had obviously been taken by surprise.

At the same time, a voice began to shout. 'Hey you! What do you think you're doing? Can't you read? Get that animal out of here.' A small, thin-faced man was racing across the yard towards her. He looked like an ageing jockey, and he was anything but pleased. 'Didn't you hear me?' he yelled. 'I said get out.'

Belinda tried to explain. 'In a minute,' she called out. 'Once the lorry's gone.'

The horses were getting spooked by all the shouting. Belinda tightened her grip on the reins.

Seconds later the lorry roared past. Almost immediately it began braking to get round the next bend. As it slowed, it backfired and a loud bang ripped through the air.

Meltdown started forward a few paces. But the other horse reared up out of control. For a moment its rider clung precariously on to its back then crashed heavily to the ground. Amongst the sound of the fall and the clattering hooves, Belinda picked out another noise. It was the sickening crack of a breaking bone.

The small man grabbed hold of the riderless horse. A second, much younger man appeared from the stable and raced to the girl who was writhing on the floor.

As the horse came under control the first man turned his attention back to Belinda. 'I don't know what you think you're up to,' he yelled angrily. 'But I can tell you now this is private property. And you are in big trouble!'

Slowly, Holly walked round the edge of the pond. 'Sit on the bench under the willow tree.' That's what Benson had said on the telephone. 'I'll meet you there at three o'clock.'

Holly hadn't expected to hear from P.J. Benson again. The phone call had taken her by surprise.

The writer's attitude was equally surprising. There was no mention of the odd behaviour at the previous meeting. It was as though nothing unusual had happened.

'I have to pop into Willow Dale tomorrow afternoon,' she'd said. 'And I thought it would give us another chance to meet up. After all, we didn't have much time the other day, did we?'

The bench under the willow tree was occupied. A smartly dressed elderly man was feeding the remains of a loaf of bread to a crowd of ducks.

Holly sat at the other end of the bench and watched the excited gaggle of birds splashing about after the floating crumbs. It was already three o'clock and there was no sign of P.J. Benson.

Holly checked the other benches around the pond. There were a few mothers with children, and couple of senior citizens passing the time of day. But no single women. *I doubt if she'll turn up while there's anyone else here*, Holly thought.

The old man's loaf of bread seemed to be lasting for ever. It was ten past three by the time he brushed the last of the crumbs from his lap and set off round the pond. The disappointed ducks splashed after him.

Almost at once there was a rustling in the branches behind the bench and a woman appeared at Holly's side. 'I thought he was never going to go,' she said. 'If he'd fed those wretched ducks much more I think they would have sunk!'

Holly knew from the voice that it was P.J. Benson. But the writer had changed her appearance yet again.

She was wearing boots, jeans and a leather jacket. All black apart from a white headscarf pulled tightly round her head. What little hair that was showing was bleached blonde and she was sporting a huge pair of pink-framed glasses.

'I know what you're thinking,' she said immediately. 'Why am I looking like this?'

'It is slightly confusing,' Holly admitted.

'There really is a very simple explanation,' Benson laughed. 'I'm a character.'

'A character?' Holly repeated.

'From my latest book. It's about two sisters with very different personalities. One of them always dresses like this. I'm spending an afternoon trying to be her. Getting to know how she feels. Does that make sense?'

Holly shrugged. 'I'm not sure.'

'It must seem a bit odd I know. But that's the way I work. I act out a lot of what happens in my books. Except the murders, that is. I find it easier to write about the characters then.'

'Is that why you changed your appearance the other day?' Holly asked. 'At the hotel?'

The writer looked uneasy. 'I'm sorry,' she said

65

softly. 'I should have warned you about that. I had to try and make myself look a little bit like the photograph on the books, otherwise word would soon get out that it was a fake. That was the best I could do. What did you think?'

'I suppose it was close enough.'

Benson looked relieved. 'Good,' she smiled. She patted Holly's hand. 'I enjoyed our meeting the other day,' she continued. 'Sorry I had to rush off so suddenly. The fact is, I was expecting a very important long-distance phone call at seven o'clock. And it had completely slipped my mind. When I realised how late it was getting I guess I panicked a little. I must've seemed very rude.'

Holly shook her head and looked away. 'Not at all,' she lied. 'I guessed it must be something like that.' Holly felt totally confused. In a few sentences the writer had turned the events of their last meeting upside down. Everything that Holly thought was strange about the writer's behaviour seemed to have been explained. Perhaps her parents were right after all. Perhaps there was no mystery to be solved.

The ducks had given up chasing the old man and were making their way back across the pond in the hope that Holly and Benson might have fresh supplies. Benson stood up. 'I hate ducks,' she said. 'Let's have a walk round the park.'

Benson linked her arm through Holly's and led

her off along one of the paths that led away from the pond. 'I've been thinking,' she said as they wound their way round the outskirts of the park. 'We'll have to set aside some time for that interview that you want to do for your school magazine.'

'Really?' Holly couldn't believe what she was hearing.

'Yes. It may not be for a couple of weeks. I am reaching quite a critical part in my book at the moment. But I think we'll definitely be able to do it sometime.'

'That would be fantastic,' said Holly.

'And then there's this Mystery Club of yours. Just maybe, if I can find time – and I'm making no promises – I might possibly be able to come along to one of the meetings.'

Holly was ecstatic. 'That really would be incredible,' she said. 'The others would love it. I know they would.'

'All right then,' Benson laughed. 'I'll see what I can do. But remember, no promises. It all depends how I get on. I've had rather a lot of interruptions to my work just recently. And that's not good.'

'That's what my dad said,' Holly grinned.

Benson looked puzzled. 'Your father?'

'It was a joke. Making out that he didn't have enough time to work because of all the interviews.'

'Sorry. I'm not with you. Does he get interviewed?'

Holly suddenly remembered. 'Of course. You don't know about it do you?'

'Know about what?'

'That radio reporter. Ainsley James. He came to interview Dad about his furniture-making.'

Holly felt Benson's grip on her arm tighten. 'Say that again,' she said.

Holly shifted uncomfortably. Benson's whole attitude had changed and the grip on her arm was starting to hurt.

'Ainsley James. He came round to interview my father yesterday morning.'

'Did he say anything about me?'

Holly tried to free her arm. 'He said he must've upset you the other day. I think he was disappointed you didn't meet him in the bar.'

'Is that all?'

'He wanted your address. To send you a cassette of the interview.'

'You didn't give it to him?'

'I don't know it,' Holly pointed out. 'He said he might be able to get it from that friend of your brother.'

Benson let go of Holly's arm and stepped backwards. Her face was taut with strain. She made a pretence of looking at her watch.

'My goodness,' she said, avoiding Holly's eyes.

68

'I hadn't realised it was that time. I've got another meeting. In town. You'll have to excuse me.' All the time she was moving away. 'I really must go!'

Holly could see her big chance slipping away again. 'What about the interview?' she said.

Benson had turned and was walking away across the grass. 'I'll be in touch,' she said over her shoulder.

Holly watched the black-clad figure in the white headscarf scurry alongside the children's play-ground. A small boy had kicked his ball over the fence surrounding the playing-area and was calling to the writer to throw it back. She seemed not to hear.

On the spur of the moment, Holly decided to follow her.

Benson had now changed direction completely and was heading back towards the main entrance. Holly knew that if she left by the near by side entrance and ran along the street, she could reach the main gates first.

A couple of minutes later she watched from behind a telephone box as the author left the park and walked along the line of parked cars. Every few metres she glanced nervously back over her shoulder.

Holly could see no sign of the silver-grey car she had ridden in a couple of days earlier. Instead Benson opened the door of a white estate car.

There was a puff of smoke from the exhaust as the engine roared into life. The next instant the car was pulling away from the kerb.

Holly stepped out into the road to try and see which way the car turned at the end of the street. There was a violent screeching of brakes, and a loud hooting of a horn. Holly turned to find herself almost on top of the dark blue bonnet of a car which had just pulled out from the kerb.

Staring in through the windscreen she could see the driver screaming at her to get out of the way. She was a woman in her late forties. She had shoulder-length fair hair and was wearing a white raincoat. Her thin, sharp features were contorted with fury.

Holly twisted sideways out of the path of the car. 'Sorry!' she tried to say to the driver. But the car was already speeding away down the street.

Holly stared after it. Her eyes scanned the number plate but it was too dirty to read accurately from that distance. But above the number plate an international car sticker was displayed. Holly could just make out enough letters to be able to guess the rest. It read 'Ecosse' – the international sign for Scotland.

Maybe she's eager to get back home, she said to herself as she reached the safety of the pavement.

And if I'm ever going to get home in one piece I'm going to have to be more careful, she said to herself. *That could have been a nasty accident.*

7 Too close for comfort

Tracy loaded another film into her camera and headed for the weights room. Photographs were going to be an important part of her holiday project and the sooner she took them the better.

Three people were working out on the equipment when Tracy entered. Two middle-aged sisters that Tracy had photographed earlier in the swimming pool. And Crawford, the Water Buffalo. The women were busy working up a sweat on two exercise bicycles, while Crawford was puffing and panting noisily backwards and forwards on a rowing machine.

'Here she is again,' said one of the women, legs pumping up and down on the pedals. 'I hope we're going to get copies of these to show our families.'

'Maybe then they'll believe that we haven't been lying around enjoying ourselves all week,' said the other.

Tracy held up the camera for them to see. 'Do you mind?' she asked.

'Not if you can make us look ten kilos lighter,' the first woman laughed.

'And ten years younger,' added the second.

'I'll do my best,' Tracy grinned.

Tracy put her eye to the viewfinder and began to focus.

There was a sudden eruption of noise from the far corner of the room. Crawford had leaped from the rowing machine and was storming towards Tracy. For a moment she thought he was going to grab the camera but instead he stalked straight past her and out the door.

'I wonder what charm school he went to?' said one of the women.

'Perhaps he's just gone to comb his hair,' said the other. 'To look his best in the photographs.'

'In that case, he doesn't need a comb. He needs a duster!'

The two women roared with laughter and Tracy clicked the shutter. It would make a good picture. But Tracy didn't join in the laughter. She had the feeling that Crawford was out to cause trouble.

By the time Tracy had finished taking photographs it was well past seven o'clock. Members were beginning to arrive at the Paradise for the evening activities. Tracy headed for the reception area to photograph people as they booked in.

On her way she stopped to look at the information board. The next night was 'Guest Night' when each member could bring along two guests free. Tracy had asked Holly and Belinda to come, and needed to check what facilities were available.

As she looked at the board she heard a familiar voice coming from reception.

'I want all calls to my room stopped for the evening, do you understand?'

'Just as you wish, Mr Crawford,' the receptionist replied.

'I really am very tired,' Crawford continued. 'I'm going back to my room now and I want to sleep straight through until the morning, so I am not to be disturbed. Not under any circumstances. No phone calls. No one knocking on the door. Nothing. Have you got that?'

'Whatever you say, sir.'

'Good.'

Tracy pretended to be examining notices as Crawford hurried past on his way to the accommodation wing. She turned and watched him go.

'Goodnight, Water Buffalo,' she said under her breath. 'Pleasant nightmares!'

Daylight was fading fast as Tracy climbed on to her bike and headed for home. She had stayed later than she had intended. She didn't have her bike lamps and would have to hurry if she was going to get back before dark.

If there had been a bus she would have left her bike at the club overnight. But Tracy knew that the last bus back into town was just after half past six. So she was surprised to see a man waiting at the bus stop a couple of hundred metres along the lane that skirted Paradise.

Maybe I should tell him the last bus has gone, Tracy thought. *Then at least he could phone for a taxi.*

There wasn't a telephone box for miles but Paradise was just a short walk across the field. He could phone from there.

The bus shelter itself was set back from the road, in the shade of overhanging trees. As Tracy drew nearer, the figure shrank further back into the shadows.

It was a mild night yet he was muffled up in a raincoat and scarf and was wearing a distinctive wide-brimmed hat.

At the last moment Tracy decided not to stop. There was something odd about the way this character was behaving. Instead she cycled straight past the bus stop and on round a bend in the road. Then she pushed her bike into the hedgerow and ran back to a point where she could have another look at the figure by the bus stop.

By that time, he had stepped forward out of the

shadows and was looking anxiously up and down the lane.

He must be waiting for something. Or someone, Tracy thought.

For a moment the man removed his hat and mopped his brow with his handkerchief. Immediately, Tracy scrabbled in her bag for her camera. Seconds later she was busy taking pictures.

From behind her she could hear the sound of a car approaching. The man heard it too. He moved forward to the edge of the footpath and looked towards the sound of the motor. Tracy hoped that he was too far away to hear the click of the camera shutter.

The car was approaching the bend fast. At the last moment the driver caught sight of Tracy and flashed the headlights in warning. For a moment she was silhouetted by the light. She saw the man at the bus stop staring hard in her direction. He must have seen her.

She pushed her camera into her bag and ran back along the road towards her bicycle. She threw her bag over her shoulder and pedalled off towards town.

Tracy's mind was buzzing. What she had seen had taken her completely by surprise. What was going on? There had to be a reason for the secrecy and the lies. But what was it?

The road into town was quiet. Pedalling along,

Tracy barely heard the car approaching from behind. It wasn't until the last moment that she realised something was wrong. By that time it was too late. It was as though the car driver hadn't seen her.

She veered towards the hedge. Luckily there was no footpath at that point. Then everything happened at once.

Her bag was ripped from her shoulder. Something on the car struck her knee. She struggled desperately to keep her balance. A moment later the wheels slid from under her and she crashed to the ground.

For a few seconds Tracy was too dazed to be certain what was going on. She heard the car skid round in the road and head back towards her. In a panic she tried to roll under the hedge. She thought the driver was trying to run her over.

Instead the car slowed to a halt further back along the road. A door opened. There were footsteps. Tracy fought to recover her senses. She lifted her head.

Outlined in the glow of the car's rear lights, a woman was kneeling down at the side of the road. She was tipping things out of Tracy's bag.

Tracy pulled herself together. 'Hey! What's the idea!' she yelled.

'Come on. Let's go!' a man's voice shouted from inside the car.

The woman threw the bag to the ground and jumped back in the car. The door slammed shut and the car roared off.

Tracy dragged herself to her feet and stumbled back towards her bag. Her foot caught something on the ground. It was the door mirror from the car. Nearby Tracy noticed something else. Her camera. Thrown clear of her bag as it crashed to the ground. She picked it up. Luckily it was still in one piece.

And so am I, she said to herself. *But only just!*

8 Stolen property

'It could have been an accident. You said yourself that it was getting dark and you hadn't got
lights.'

'If it was an accident why come back and go
through my bag?'

Holly and Tracy were drinking fruit cocktails in
the juice bar at Paradise.

'She could have panicked. Thought you were
badly injured and been looking for something with
your name and address on.'

'And then disappeared when I shouted out? No
way.' Tracy had no doubt. She'd been deliberately
forced off the road. And she knew who was behind
it. Crawford.

'You've no proof he was in the car,' Holly
pointed out.

'He was at the bus stop. He had different glasses
and what looked like a moustache. But I recognised
him the minute he took his hat off.' Tracy patted her
camera. 'And I've got the pictures to prove it.'

'But what was he doing?'

'Waiting for somebody to pick him up.'

Holly sucked thoughtfully on her straw. 'That doesn't mean to say he was in the car.'

'I heard his voice, remember,' said Tracy.

Holly picked out a slice of kiwi fruit that was floating in her glass and began to nibble at it. 'Of course, there's no reason why he shouldn't go out. It's not a prison camp.'

'Then why make such a big thing about going to bed and not being disturbed?' Tracy argued. 'No. He knew he was going out all along. But he wanted everybody to think he was still in his room. Then, when he realised that I'd seen him, he panicked.'

Holly fished out a slice of apple. 'But you wouldn't recognise the woman again?'

Tracy shook her head. 'It was too dark. I think she had long hair. Light-coloured clothes. But really I was too dazed to know.'

'What about the car?'

It was a dark colour. Green. Blue. Black. Any of those. And now it's got a door mirror missing.'

Holly stared into her glass. 'I still don't see a reason.'

'And I don't see a reason why Benson should freak out on you like she did in the park. I guess we'll just have to work on them.' Tracy drained the last of her drink. 'Then there's the other mystery,' she added.

'What's that?'

'Where's Belinda? She's three quarters of an hour late.'

The plan had been for the Mystery Club to meet in the reception area at six thirty. Tracy's idea was a sauna followed by a swim in the pool. 'Sounds all right to me,' Belinda had said. 'A sauna is my kind of exercise.' But when she still hadn't turned up by quarter to seven Holly and Tracy decided to get a drink.

'Maybe she's been kidnapped,' Holly suggested. 'By whom?'

'P.J. Benson and the Water Buffalo.'

Tracy took a deep breath. 'I don't think so,' she said quietly. 'Because *he's* just walked in!

Holly looked round. The Water Buffalo wasn't hard to spot. There was nobody else about. He was standing at the counter. He had his back to Holly and Tracy but it was clear that he was in a temper. He rang the bell for service. Then he rang again. Holding it down for several seconds. Nobody came.

With a gasp of exasperation he turned round. His eyes settled on Tracy, but his face showed nothing. It was impossible to tell what he was thinking. Tracy stared back. The battle of wills was only broken by the arrival of Steve Biggins behind the counter.

Crawford began complaining loudly about the lack of service. But his voice was drowned out by an announcement on the Tannoy. 'Tracy Foster to reception please.'

'That must be Belinda,' said Tracy.

Holly began collecting her belongings together but Tracy stopped her. 'Leave everything here,' she said. 'They'll be all right. And Belinda's bound to want to take fuel on board before exerting herself in the sauna.'

They found Belinda slumped on a chair near the reception desk.

'What's the matter with you?' said Tracy. 'Hard day at the freezer?'

'I wish!' said Belinda. 'I've just finished work.'

'Work?' Holly echoed. 'What work?'

Belinda screwed up her face. 'Hmm!' she said. 'It's a long story. Let's go somewhere we can get an ice-cream and I'll fill you in.'

'Forget ice-cream,' said Tracy. 'This is a health club. They don't allow such things. Think healthy fruit cocktail instead!'

Belinda made the most of her story. It spread over two Tropical Sunrises. She told all about her ride over to Hanover Hall, the men in the wood, the red van, the backfiring lorry, and finished off with a graphic description of the sound of breaking bones.

'I still don't see why the stable girl breaking her arm means that you've got to take over her work,' said Holly.

'For no money! That's what gets me,' Belinda moaned. 'I have to do it for no money!'

'But why?'

Belinda fished into her drink, chasing an elusive grape. 'You know what my mother's like. She was furious. She said it was all my fault. That it was private property and I shouldn't have ridden in there in the first place. And that I wasn't fit to be out on the road, and we'd probably end up getting sued for thousands of pounds. So to try and get round them she phoned up and said I'd do it for nothing until the other girl's arm was mended.'

'You did say you wanted to get a closer look at the Blushing Bride,' Tracy grinned. 'Now you're doing it!'

Belinda flicked the grape into the air and caught it in her mouth. 'I suppose you two have just been sitting around enjoying yourselves,' she complained.

'Have we got news for you!' said Holly.

Tracy stood up. 'We'll bring you up to date in the sauna,' she said. She started to collect her things together. Suddenly she stopped. 'My camera! It's gone. It's been stolen!'

The camera had disappeared without a trace. It wasn't where Tracy had left it. It hadn't got mixed up with Holly or Belinda's things. It hadn't been handed in at reception.

It was only when they found Steve Biggins that any light was thrown on the matter.

'Your camera?' he said. 'Where did you leave it?'

'In the juice bar while we went to get Belinda from reception. Did you see anybody take it?'

Steve looked uneasy. 'I left once I'd served Crawford. We're short-staffed tonight and I'm trying to do three jobs at once.'

'So you've no idea where it might have got to?'

Steve was nervous about something. He dropped his voice. 'Look, I've got to be careful. I can't go round making accusations. I could get sacked for that.'

It was obvious that Steve was holding something back.

'Come on, Steve,' said Holly. 'We won't tell anybody.'

Steve thought for a moment before speaking. 'OK!' he said at last. 'But don't let on I told you. I went over to the accomodation block to replace a light bulb. On the way back I passed Crawford in the corridor. He was carrying a camera.'

'I knew it!' said Tracy. 'He's stolen it. Well, he's not going to get away with it!' She turned on her heel and began to walk away.

Steve grabbed her arm. 'Wait!' he said. 'I just said he was carrying a camera. It didn't have to be yours. It could have been his own.'

'Then let's ask him,' said Tracy. 'What's his room number?'

'Seventeen. But he's not there. He's in the swimming pool.'

'So much the better,' said Tracy.

Steve let go of her arm. 'I don't think I want to know any more about this,' he said.

The Mystery Club was standing in the accommodation block. Room seventeen was at the end of a long corridor next to a fire exit. 'If you wait here,' Tracy instructed Belinda, 'and look through this window, you'll be able to see Crawford coming back from the pool. As soon as you see him, whistle.'

'Any particular tune?' said Belinda.

'Just whistle. Then walk down there and get in his way. Slow him down a bit. We'll get out through the fire exit.'

'I'm not sure about this.' Holly was looking worried. 'Going into his room.'

'Are you kidding?' Tracy snapped. 'He knocks me off my bike. Almost kills me. Now he's stolen my camera. What else does he have to do? Besides, we're only going to get my camera back.'

'Tracy's right,' said Belinda. 'She's only going to take back what's hers.'

'If it's there!' Holly pointed out.

'It's there all right.' Tracy was already heading along the corridor.

'Just a minute,' Holly hissed after her. 'How are we going to get in?'

Tracy turned round and held up her plastic membership card. 'Never seen them use one of these in the films?'

Tracy pushed the card in between the door-frame and the lock and jiggled it about. Nothing happened. She tried again in a slightly different place. Still nothing. 'The lock just slips back,' she explained to Holly. 'It always works.'

'In the films!' Holly scoffed.

'Try pushing the door while I'm doing it,' said Tracy. 'Maybe that will make a difference.'

Holly grabbed hold of the handle and pushed. The handle clicked downwards and the door swung open. She gave Tracy a withering look. 'It wasn't even locked,' she said.

For such an expensive club, the room was nothing special. It was small and neat but hardly luxurious. At first glance, there weren't too many places to hide a camera.

'You take the dressing-table, I'll go through the chest of drawers,' said Tracy.

Holly started from the bottom and worked her way up. The bottom two drawers contained only clothes. It was the top drawer which surprised her. 'Hey!' she called to Tracy. 'Come and look at this.'

Tracy let out a long, low whistle.

Inside the drawer, there were two wigs with different lengths of hair, a packet of hair dye and boxes of stage make-up. There was a false beard and moustache, a bottle of spirit gum and several pairs of glasses in different styles.

'Now tell me he's not up to something,' said Tracy. 'Here's his disguise kit.'

Holly pushed the drawer shut. 'It's not your camera though, is it?' she said. She opened the bedside cabinet. It was empty apart from a few simple medicines. 'Nothing here. How about you?' she said.

Tracy shook her head. 'Nothing.' She looked round the room. 'I'll check the wardrobe.'

Tracy pulled open the wardrobe doors. Two or three suits and a jacket were hung inside. Besides those there were shelves neatly stacked with shirts, jumpers and socks.

Carefully Tracy removed the jumpers to check behind. There was nothing there. But as she replaced them something caught her eye. 'Look at this!' she called to Holly.

Holly hurried over. Her eyes widened. The top jumper was plain blue. But on the left breast was a white monogram. It read simply, 'Mike'.

'If his name is Peter, somebody can't spell,' said Tracy.

'No sign of the camera though. And we'd better get going,' said Holly nervously.

'Wait!' Tracy was staring down beneath the suits. 'What's that?'

At the bottom of the wardrobe there was a large book lying at an awkward angle. Holly knelt down and read out the title. *Tomb Treasures of Ancient Egypt*.

Tracy pushed Holly out of the way and shoved her hand under the book. A moment later she was waving her camera in the air.

'Didn't I tell you?' she yelled. 'He did steal it!'

But Holly had seen something else. Next to the wardrobe was a waste paper bin. And in the bottom of the bin was a long length of exposed film. Holly lifted it out and held it in front of Tracy. 'Check the camera,' she told her.

A look of despair came over Tracy's face. 'It's empty,' she said. 'He's exposed the film. The photos are ruined.'

It was then that they heard Belinda whistle.

The two girls dived for the door. In the corridor, Holly reached out to open the fire exit door. But Tracy grabbed hold of her arm.

'Wait!' she said. There was panic in her eyes. 'My membership card! I don't have it. I must have left it in there.'

'Then leave it,' said Holly. 'There's no time to get it now. He's on his way. You'll get caught.'

Tracy opened the door to the room. 'If I leave it

behind he'll know I've been in there. It won't take me a second.'

Holly watched the door close behind Tracy. In the distance, she heard the sound of something crashing to the floor. Belinda was clearly doing her stuff to delay Crawford.

There was a confusion of voices. Then Crawford's bellow echoed along the corridors. 'For goodness sake get out the way, you stupid girl!'

There was no sign of Tracy. And Crawford was on his way again. A few seconds more and he would turn the corner. Holly opened the fire exit door. She paused. Still no Tracy. She had to go. There was no point in both of them getting caught, she thought. Holly stepped out into the cool night air and closed the door behind her. She waited for the explosion of shouting that would show that Tracy had been caught red-handed.

On the inside she heard the footsteps grow louder. Then the click of the handle as the door to Crawford's room opened and shut. Then – nothing.

Perhaps Tracy was hiding in the bathroom. Or under the bed. Or in the wardrobe. Wherever it was she was bound to be found sooner or later. Holly strained her ears. But all she could hear was the sound of the breeze in the trees.

Then a voice spoke behind her. 'Waiting for somebody?'

Holly spun round to see Tracy's grinning face poking round the corner of the wall. 'Good thing there was a window,' she said. 'Otherwise I might just have been caught!'

9 Taken by surprise

'Excuse me. I'm looking for a book by P.J. Benson.'

The Mystery Club was trying to recover from the excitement of the night before in the quiet of the Willow Dale library.

The librarian glanced up briefly from her work. 'They'll be over there. Under "Mysteries". If we have any in; they're very popular.'

Belinda looked across at Tracy and shook her head despairingly.

'The thing is,' said Holly politely, 'this is a special book: *Death Takes A Holiday*. I've looked it up on the computer and you've got it. But the entry says "For Reference Only". I think it's because it's a first edition.'

A look of recognition spread across the librarian's face. 'Oh, I see,' she said. 'I'm afraid you can't take that out then. I'm sure we've got later editions you can borrow.'

Belinda rolled her eyes up towards the ceiling and sighed. Tracy moved uneasily away. If Belinda was going to explode she didn't want to be too close.

Holly nodded understandingly. 'We know that,' she said. 'But we've been told there's something different about the first edition and we'd like to check it out. Could we have a quick look?'

The librarian put down her pen. 'I'm sorry,' she said. 'Books like that are kept in a special store away from the main library. The earliest I can get it is tomorrow afternoon.'

'I don't believe it,' Belinda snapped. 'Isn't this supposed to be a public service?'

Tracy grabbed her by the arm and frog-marched her away. The librarian watched her go with a stunned expression on her face.

'You'll have to excuse my friend,' Holly apologised. 'Tomorrow afternoon will be fine.'

'What if it had been an emergency?' said Belinda, slicing open a fruit scone. 'Something we needed urgently?'

'Well, it wasn't,' said Holly. 'So tomorrow afternoon is soon enough.'

The Mystery Club had adjourned to Annie's Tea-room where they were tucking into mid-morning snacks. At the same time, Holly was leafing through a book she had just borrowed from the library.

'What is that anyway?' said Belinda.

Holly showed Belinda the cover. 'It's the same book that was in Crawford's wardrobe.'

'*Tomb Treasures of Ancient Egypt*! Since when have

you been interested in them?'

'Since I wanted to find out more about Crawford,' Holly replied. 'I mean, don't you find it a little bit strange that somebody as pig-ignorant as he is should be interested in something like this?'

'Not a bit,' said Belinda. 'He reminds me of a mummy anyway.'

'I still think a water buffalo is better,' Holly grinned.

'A mummified water buffalo?' Belinda suggested.

'Never mind about that.' Tracy pushed her plate away. 'We've got work to do!'

Holly snapped the book shut. 'You're right,' she said. She opened her bag and took out the red notebook that the Mystery Club used to keep notes about all their cases. 'Where do we start?'

Tracy had no doubt. 'Crawford! Or whatever his name is.'

'The Water Buffalo!' Belinda grinned. 'Just call him that.'

'Whatever we call him,' said Holly, 'He's definitely up to something. But what?'

'Three things to note down,' said Tracy. 'He's probably using a false name. He's having meetings that he doesn't want anybody to know about. And he's got everything he needs to make a disguise.'

Holly put down the pen. 'What does that add up to?' she wondered.

'He's on the run,' said Belinda. 'From the police.

For fraud. Armed robbery. Murder!'

'Maybe he's escaped from jail,' Tracy suggested. 'And he's hiding out.'

Holly wrote it down. 'They're both possibilities,' she admitted. 'But why the secret meeting?'

'Could be that somebody is going to smuggle him out of the country,' said Tracy. 'Or maybe somebody is blackmailing him.'

Holly added it to the list. 'So what do we do?'

'There's not much we can do,' said Tracy. 'Just keep a close eye on him. Steve Biggins has promised to help. He's a bit jumpy but he says he'll let me know about anything that happens when I'm not there. So between us we should have him fully covered.'

Holly made a note and turned the page. 'That's Crawford then. For now. That brings us to—'

'My two men in the wood,' Belinda interrupted.

'What sort of story is that?' Tracy scoffed. 'A couple of bird-watchers pitch a tent in the wood. Big deal. Forget them. Let's concentrate on Benson, the mysterious mystery writer. If that's who she is.'

'We should know once we've seen that first edition,' said Holly. 'If there really is no picture on the back, which is what she said, then I'd say we can be pretty sure it's P.J. Benson all right.'

'In which case, end of mystery!' Belinda snapped. If the others were going to ignore her mystery then she was going to ignore theirs.

Holly closed the red notebook and leaned back in her chair. 'I wish it was as simple as that,' she said. 'But I just feel there's something wrong.'

'What?' demanded Belinda.

'I don't know,' Holly had to admit. 'She's just acting strange.'

'Talking about strange,' said Tracy, 'what's going on outside?'

It sounded as though a pack of wild animals were clumping along the pavement outside. The hoots and screeches grew louder and a moment later Holly's worst fears were realised as Jamie and three of his friends fell through the door.

Jamie immediately headed in the direction of the Mystery Club. 'I thought I'd find you here,' he said.

'Well you've found me,' Holly whispered through gritted teeth. 'Now go away.'

'I will,' said Jamie. 'Once I've given you this.'

He placed a flat brown-paper parcel in front of Holly. She eyed it suspiciously. 'What is it?'

'I dunno. A taxi delivered it to the house. Just after you'd gone.'

'A taxi?'

'Yeah. Dad thought it might be important and asked me to bring it in to you. So I did. Out of the kindness of my heart,' he said mockingly. 'And because he gave me these.'

Jamie laid two pound coins down next to the

parcel. Immediately one of the other boys grabbed them and headed for the door with Jamie in hot pursuit. 'Oh, no you don't,' he was shouting. 'Give them back!'

'Hey wait a minute,' Holly cried. 'Did the taxi driver say anything?' But it was too late. Her brother and his friends had gone as quickly as they had come.

Holly, Tracy and Belinda sat looking at the parcel. 'Holly Adams. Personal' was written across it in black felt-tip pen.

'Oh well,' said Holly. 'Only one way to find out.'

It was the work of a few moments to undo the parcel. As the brown paper was pulled away the cover of a book became visible.

Holly read out the title. *'Death Takes a Holiday* by P.J. Benson. It's the first edition!' She turned the book over. There was no photograph on the back cover.

'Looks like we've got our answer,' said Tracy.

'We've got more than that,' Belinda said.

A single sheet of writing-paper had slipped out of the book. Holly turned it over. She read the message and whistled in amazement.

'She certainly knows how to take you by surprise,' she said.

The bank where Holly's mother was manager was

only a short walk away from the library. Tracy and Belinda talked excitedly as they made their way through the streets towards it. But Holly was deep in thought. She couldn't get Benson's note out of her mind.

Dear Holly, it had begun. *Here is the book that I promised you. Now do you believe who I am? I've been thinking about that meeting with the Mystery Club. I have to visit St Ethelred's Church at Witney Harrows tomorrow (more research!) Could you all meet me there at three o'clock? Then afterwards perhaps I could take the three of you for a bite to eat? Look forward to seeing you there. Benson.*

The Mystery Club had to look up Witney Harrows on a map in the library. It was little more than a collection of farms scattered around an isolated church about ten kilometres out of town.

How would they get there? Going by bike would lead to difficulties if Benson really did take them somewhere for a meal. Then Holly remembered. Her mother was going to an area meeting of branch managers. Perhaps she could drop them off on the way. So they were on their way to the bank to ask.

'Just look at all these cars,' said Holly. The traffic outside the bank was almost at a standstill. A traffic warden was trying to clear a blockage at the end of the street caused by a coach which was having difficulty making a right turn.

'Belinda!' A man's voice called over the noise of the engines. 'Belinda, over here!'

A maroon Mercedes was parked a few metres away from the entrance to the bank. A tall figure that looked as though he hadn't eaten or slept for a week was standing by the half open driver's door. He was waving vigorously at Belinda. Belinda peered through her glasses for a moment and then waved back.

'It's Greg!' she said.

'Who's Greg?' said Tracy.

'From the stables. He helps look after the Blushing Bride.'

'Don't tell me he's the best man!' Tracy joked.

But Belinda was already jogging along the street towards the gleaming Mercedes.

'What are you doing here?' she asked Greg after the others had caught up and she had introduced them.

'Mr Shah had to come to the bank,' said Greg. 'They're probably trying to borrow money off him or something like that.'

'Who's Mr Shah?' asked Holly.

'He owns the Blushing Bride,' Belinda replied before Greg could speak.

'So why do you have to drive him?' said Tracy. 'Doesn't he have his own car?'

Greg looked from Tracy to Belinda. 'Is she joking?' he said. Then before anybody could answer,

'This *is* his car. I'm just driving it. Mine's a wreck. Mr Shah wouldn't be seen dead in it. Anyway, he likes to be driven. That way he doesn't waste time. He just carries on making phone calls.'

'Who's looking after the Bride then?'

Greg obviously appreciated her concern. 'Don't worry. Hinkley is there.'

'Hinkley?' Tracy repeated.

'He's the Head Lad. Though all he does most of the time is get his orders from the boss and pass them on to me.'

'And me!' said Belinda.

The traffic warden had solved the coach problem and was walking slowly back along the street towards them.

'I think you're about to get booked,' said Holly. 'You're on a double yellow line.'

Greg pulled a parking ticket out of his pocket. 'We've been booked already. Mr Shah would rather pay fines than walk.' Suddenly Greg scrambled round to the pavement and opened the rear door. 'Look out,' he said, under his voice. 'Here he comes!'

The man descending the steps of the bank had the kind of easy confidence that goes with lots of money. A dark grey overcoat was slung carelessly across his shoulders. Beneath it he wore a silk pinstripe suit. The swarthy skin, black hair and deep dark eyes suggested Mediterranean origins.

But when he spoke his accent was impeccable English.

'Sorry to break up the party, but I'm in a rush.' He slipped a brown leather brief-case on to the back seat then slid in beside it. His eyes rested briefly on Belinda and he gave a slight nod of recognition as Greg closed the door. The next moment, Mr Shah had picked up the car telephone and was punching in a number.

'See you tomorrow, Belinda,' said Greg as he climbed into the driving seat. 'Bye, girls.'

Holly, Tracy and Belinda stood outside the bank and waved as the car pulled out into the traffic. Shah was already deep in telephone conversation. Holly turned to enter the bank but was knocked backwards as the door opened and someone raced out. The figure hurtled down the steps and along the street towards a red transit van which was already pulling out into the stream of cars.

Holly twisted round just in time to see a man with a grey pony-tail climbing up into the van's passenger seat. A flurry of horns sounded behind the van. The next moment it had accelerated along the street and turned out of sight.

'Well, what do you think about that?' said Holly. 'Some people!' She turned to Tracy.

But Tracy was looking at Belinda, who was pointing after the van in wonder.

'That was them!' she gasped finally.
'Who?' said Holly and Tracy.
'The men in the wood. They're following Mr Shah!'

10   Is anybody there?

Belinda unclipped her seat-belt and opened the car door.

'And another thing,' said Mrs Hayes. 'Do what you're told. You're there to work don't forget.'

'Without pay!' muttered Belinda.

'What was that?'

'I said without play. I'll work without play. Non-stop.'

'I should hope so,' said Mrs Hayes, patting her immaculately styled hair. 'We're lucky Mr Shah's not taking us to court.'

Belinda reached in and grabbed hold of her bag. 'Just one thing,' she said.

'What is it now?' Mrs Hayes sighed. 'I've got my Cordon Bleu cookery class at ten o'clock.'

'I'm just reminding you. I might be late back tonight,' said Belinda. 'We're having a Mystery Club outing.'

Mrs Hayes nodded and put the car into gear. 'Just as long as you don't need a lift,' she said as she glanced in the mirror. 'It's my badminton night.'

Belinda shut the door and the car pulled away.

It was unusually quiet in the stable yard. Nothing seemed to be happening at all. All the doors were still firmly shut. There was no movement and no noise.

Belinda tried the door to the Blushing Bride's stable. It was bolted on the inside.

Belinda looked around. She suddenly realised that she had no idea where Greg and Hinkley were living. She supposed they must sleep up at the Hall but no one had actually said.

She turned back to the stable door and hammered on it with the flat of her hand. Perhaps Greg was out exercising the Blushing Bride. From inside she heard the racehorse whinny and shift around uneasily. Another theory bit the dust.

She was about to set off on the long walk to the Hall when she heard the clatter of bolts. A moment later the stable door opened. A very dishevelled Greg stood blinking in the sunlight. His clothes were dusty and there were bits of straw sticking out everywhere. He looked like a scarecrow. There was a puzzled look on his face.

'What are you doing here so early?' he said with a yawn.

'Early? What are you talking about? It's almost ten o'clock.'

Greg slumped sideways against the doorpost.

'Oh, no, I must have overslept. I'd better get moving before Hinkley turns up.' He disappeared back into the darkness of the stable. Belinda followed him in.

Greg was stumbling around in the far corner of the stable looking for his boots. A sleeping-bag was laid out on a pile of straw. A torch and an alarm clock with a cracked face were lying on a wooden chair pushed back against the wall.

'What's going on? Are you sleeping in here?' Belinda asked. Greg nodded. 'Sort of.'

'Sort of?'

'That is – yes. But not every night.'

'No room at the Hall?'

'Plenty of room. But . . .' Greg's voice trailed away.

'But what?'

Greg ran a hand through his hair and chewed at his bottom lip. 'Wait there,' he told Belinda. He shuffled over to the stable door and checked outside. Satisfied there was nobody there, he turned back to Belinda. 'I shouldn't be telling you this.'

Belinda's pulse quickened. 'You can trust me,' she said quietly.

Greg weighed it over in his mind. 'All right then,' he said finally. 'You're bound to find out sooner or later anyway. Somebody's trying to nobble the Blushing Bride.'

'Nobble her?'

'Get to her. Fix her.'

'But why?'

'Next month she's down to run in the Prince of Wales' Gold Trophy. She's almost bound to win. Only one other horse has any chance at all. Rain Dance. If they can get the Blushing Bride out of the race then people who've backed Rain Dance will stand to win a lot of money. That's why Mr Shah's brought us out here. Right away from everywhere. It's safer.'

Belinda's eyes were alight with excitement. 'Who's doing it?' she asked. She was thinking of the men in the red van.

'We don't know,' Greg said. 'Mr Shah had a tip off a couple of weeks ago. That's why there was such a rush moving in here.'

'Right,' said Belinda. The mystery was shaping up nicely. 'But what's that got to do with you sleeping in the stable?'

Greg had found his boots and was struggling to pull them on. 'We have to make sure nobody gets to the Bride in the night. Jackie and I were supposed to take turns. Until she broke her wrist. Then Mr Shah told Hinkley he'd have to do it instead. But most nights he's out drinking and doesn't get back till next morning.'

'What's going on here?' a voice snapped out.

Belinda spun round in alarm. The Blushing Bride shifted uneasily. In the doorway, silhouetted

105

against the bright light streaming in from outside, stood Mr Shah.

'I asked what's going on? Greg?'

'Er . . . we're running a bit behind this morning I'm afraid, Mr Shah.'

'I can see that. I'd like a word, please.' The racehorse owner turned on his heel and walked towards the middle of the yard.

Reluctantly Greg followed. 'Wish me luck,' he whispered to Belinda. 'I'll need it.'

Greg approached his boss as though he were on his way to face a firing squad.

Shah's face showed no emotion as Greg shuffled towards him. Only the fingers of his right hand tapping impatiently against the side of his leg betrayed his anger. As Greg reached him, Shah took hold of his arm and began to lead him away. Before they had taken more than few steps a car roared recklessly into the yard and screeched to a halt just a few metres away from them.

The two men twisted round in alarm just in time to see Hinkley stumble out from the passenger seat. Almost immediately the car reversed round and shot back on to the road in a cloud of dust.

'Where have you been?' Shah snapped. 'I thought it was your turn to be here last night.'

Hinkley licked his lips nervously. But before he could speak Shah stopped him.

'Never mind. This place is a shambles. I want to

talk to both of you. Now. Over at the Hall.' The racehorse owner looked back towards the stables. 'Belinda!' he shouted out.

Belinda hurried forward to the doorway.

'Get things moving here, will you? Greg will be back in an hour.' With that he turned and strode off towards the Hall with Greg and Hinkley trailing behind.

By the time Greg got back, Belinda had fed and watered the horse and started to clear out the stable.

'You've done well,' said Greg. He had a smile on his face.

'What are you so pleased about?' said Belinda. 'I thought you were really in for it.'

'So did I,' Greg admitted. 'But it was Hinkley who got it in the neck. I think the boss must have heard me telling you about him staying away most nights.'

'Serves him right,' said Belinda.

'He's bound to blame me though,' said Greg. 'And he'll find some way of getting his own back. You can be sure of that. And I didn't get off scot-free with Shah either,' he added. 'He's coming back this afternoon to check everything over. It has to be just right or there'll be more trouble.'

'Don't worry,' said Belinda, picking up a broom

and starting to sweep. 'I'll stay on till it's all finished.'

'Oh, by the way,' said Greg, giving Belinda a smile of gratitude, 'the boss said Hinkley has got to sleep here for the next three nights to make up for what he's missed. So that gives me a bit of free time. So I was wondering if you and your friends would like to come over tomorrow night. We could have a barbecue down by the river.'

Belinda's face lit up. 'That would be great, she said. 'Now let's get to work. There's a lot to be done, and I'm supposed to be somewhere else this afternoon.'

St Ethelred's Church, Witney Harrows, stood high on a hill. There were no other buildings within a kilometre of it. A lane, little more than a cart-track, ran up to it. At the bottom, next to the bleak grave-yard, there was a tiny parking area. St Ethelred's congregation was either very small or very fond of walking.

Mrs Adams turned the car round and switched off the engine. 'Doesn't look like she's here yet. There's no car. What do you want to do?'

'We'll wait,' said Holly, opening the passenger door.

'Thanks for the lift,' said Tracy, jumping out the other side. Belinda hadn't turned up. Neither of them knew why.

'Sorry I hadn't got time to go looking for Belinda,' said Mrs Adams.

'That's OK,' said Holly. 'She must have got held up. I'm sure she'll find her way here somehow.'

Holly and Tracy waved as the car pulled away.

'So where is she?' said Tracy.

'You know what she's like when she gets round horses. She loses all track of time.'

'I wasn't talking about Belinda,' said Tracy. 'I meant Benson! The mystery writer!'

Holly pushed open the porch gate. 'Don't worry,' she said. 'She'll turn up. The only thing I don't know is whether I'll recognise her or not when she does!'

St Ethelred's Church was very plain and very simple. No soaring spire. No stained-glass windows. Just a stone-built nave with a square, squat bell-tower.

Inside it was dark. Very dark. There was one small rectangular window high above the altar and a couple of smaller ones on each side wall. But the light from them made very little difference.

'What do you think?' whispered Tracy.

'I think it's dark!' said Holly.

Tracy pushed her forward and stepped in behind her. As she let go of the door it slammed shut.

'There must be a through draught.' Tracy hadn't expected that.

'How can there be?' said Holly. 'This is the only door.'

Feeling their way in the dark, they inched down the centre aisle. As they neared the altar, Holly stopped to sniff the air.

'I can smell smoke,' she said quietly.

'So can I,' Tracy agreed. She stepped forward and pointed at the altar. 'Look,' she said. 'That candle has just been put out.' A faint plume of smoke was rising up from the wick. 'Somebody's been in here!'

A door creaked and the plume of smoke shivered.

Holly twisted round. 'There's your draught,' she whispered. 'It must be the door to the bell-tower.'

Tracy took a deep breath. 'In that case whoever put out the candle must be up there.'

'After you,' said Holly, pushing Tracy forward.

With the door to the bell-tower fully open, Holly and Tracy could feel air from above on their faces.

A set of stone steps was built into the wall of the tower. They were steep and damp and barely wide enough for one person to climb. It was even darker than the church itself.

Holly poked Tracy in the back. 'Go on,' she whispered. 'I'll keep watch down here.'

'You will not!' Tracy reached back and grabbed hold of Holly's wrist. 'If the Hunchback of Notre

110

Dame is up there with the bells, you're going to meet him too!'

They climbed upwards one step at a time, slowly feeling their way in the dark. The stairs were treacherous. Besides being slippery each one was a different height. It would have been all too easy to miss a foothold and crash to the bottom.

'Almost there!' said Tracy as they neared the top. It was getting lighter again. A few steps more and the stairs opened out on to a platform. Inside, in the great hollow of the tower hung two large bells. To the outside there was a low parapet wall with a large opening above it. The view was spectacular. You could see for miles across the countryside.

Tracy leaned against the wall and gulped in the fresh air. 'Not much chance of anybody sneaking up on you here,' she said. 'You can see for ever.'

Holly put her arm round Tracy's shoulders. 'So where's the mysterious candle-snuffer then? Hiding in the bells?'

Tracy pushed Holly's arm away. She never liked being wrong. 'At least I wasn't afraid to lead the way,' she said.

'You don't think I was really afraid!' said Holly.

'If you weren't you did a darned good impression.' Tracy let her eyes wander lazily over the landscape spread out in front of her. 'Beautiful!' she said, turning back to examine the bells. A moment later her scream shattered the calm of the countryside.

11 A quick disappearance

'Tracy Foster, this is P.J. Benson.' Holly made the introductions.

'I really am very sorry,' the writer apologised. I didn't mean to frighten you.'

'Well, you did. Suddenly appearing like that, without warning. I thought you were a ghost or something! All I could see was your face.'

'I didn't realise my face was so scary.' Benson tried to make a joke but Tracy wasn't amused.

'What were you doing anyway, sneaking up on us like that?'

'I'm sure Benson didn't mean to frighten you,' said Holly. In truth she was feeling a bit shaky herself. But more from the effects of Tracy's screams than the sudden, unannounced appearance of Benson at the top of the stairway. Though appearing out of the gloom and dressed in black the writer had looked a little bit ghostly.

'I still don't see what you were up to,' said Tracy.

Benson looked uneasy. 'Research, I'm afraid,' she apologised. 'It's a bad habit of mine.'

'Research?' Tracy echoed.

'How do you mean?' said Holly.

'An incident in the book I'm writing is set in an isolated church. That's why I came out here. To soak up the atmosphere. Anyway, the murderer lures a private detective out to the church to try and get rid of him. While I was waiting for you I thought of a way he might do it. I couldn't resist trying it out.'

Holly was already thinking it through. 'So the smoking candle and the open door to the tower were part of it.'

Benson's eyes lit up. 'You've got it,' she said. 'I guessed that a real investigator wouldn't be able to resist clues like that. So I set them up, hid myself away and waited to see what happened. Then all I had to do was sneak up behind you and push you out of the tower.'

'Well at least you spared us that bit,' said Tracy.

Benson offered Tracy her hand. 'Am I forgiven?'

'I reckon so.' Tracy shook her hand. 'I've read some of your books. But I never thought I'd be helping you write one. Do I get a credit?'

Benson started to laugh. 'I'll make sure of it.' She linked arms with the two girls and gazed out over the countryside. 'I'm glad you could come,' she said. 'But I thought there were three of you.'

'Belinda didn't turn up,' said Holly. 'She must have got sidetracked.'

'Side-saddled more like,' said Tracy. 'She's a horse nut and—'

Tracy stopped mid-sentence. A look of panic had spread across Benson's face. Her eyes were staring madly ahead. 'What is it? What's wrong?' Tracy asked.

'Nothing,' Benson gasped. But her face told a different story.

Tracy looked at Holly, who nodded towards the lane that led to the church. A car was speeding along it. Benson seemed transfixed by the sight of the approaching vehicle. She was unaware of anything else.

The driver hit the brakes at the last minute and the car slewed to a halt just centimetres from the porch gate. A second later the passenger door opened and a pale rather shaken figure climbed out.

'It's Belinda!' yelled Tracy. 'Hey! We're up here!'

'Hold on,' shouted Holly. 'We're coming down!'

As Holly turned towards the staircase Benson slumped against the wall in relief. 'Are you OK?' Holly asked.

'I'm fine,' Benson smiled weakly. 'Just a little faint. I think it's time the four of us got some food.'

The Three Horseshoes was a well-known and very expensive restaurant set high on the moors outside

Willow Dale. Nobody had argued with Benson when she suggested that they travel there to eat.

They'd had to walk to Benson's car which was parked on an even smaller road about a kilometre away from the church. 'I always was hopeless at map-reading,' she'd said by way of explanation.

The drive to the Three Horseshoes took a good half hour. Belinda filled in the time by telling them what had been happening at Hanover Hall.

'Of course,' she'd said finally as they approached the restaurant, 'if Greg hadn't given me a lift over in his old banger, I'd have missed out on this altogether.'

'You still might miss out on it,' said Holly. 'They probably won't let you in dressed like that!'

Belinda was wearing her usual combination of jeans and faded green sweat-shirt. 'What do you expect? I've come straight from work,' she said.

'You look fine,' Benson told her. 'And anyway, the more expensive the place the less bothered they are how you look.'

As they entered the restaurant, Tracy pulled Holly to one side. 'Did you see it?' she whispered urgently.

'See what?' Holly didn't have a clue what Tracy was talking about.

'There was a car. A couple of hundred metres behind us. It picked us up near the church and followed us all the way here.'

'Where is it now?'

'I just caught a glimpse of it flash past after we'd turned into the carpark.'

'It is a main road,' Holly pointed out. 'Lots of cars come this way.'

'It was a dark blue saloon.'

Holly pursed her lips. 'Did you see the driver?'

Tracy shook her head. 'Too far away.'

'Well a keep quiet about it,' Holly told her. 'Now come on. We're getting left behind.'

The next few hours sped past. The food was fantastic, with helpings big enough to defeat everyone but Belinda. Though even she refused second helpings of Italian ice-cream cake. But better even than the meal was the conversation.

Benson wanted to know everything there was to know about the Mystery Club. She listened avidly to the tales of their past adventures. Sometimes she was able to work out what was behind the mystery before they'd finished the story. But at other times she was just as foxed as they had been. Finally, Tracy brought her up to date by telling her all about the events at Paradise.

'This Crawford fellow certainly seems like a strange character,' Benson admitted as she paid the bill. 'But there could be a perfectly reasonable explanation for it all.'

'Like what?' said Tracy.

'That I don't know. Nor can I tell you what's going on over at Hanover Hall. But what I do know is this: most real-life mysteries have perfectly innocent explanations.'

'Not with us,' said Belinda.

Benson led the way back to the car. Twilight had already set in. And in the distance they could see the lights of Willow Dale. Holly stood looking out over the town. It had been a fascinating afternoon. But there was one mystery that hadn't been mentioned during the course of the meal. That was the mystery of P.J. Benson herself. Earlier that afternoon, the sight of Greg's car approaching the church had almost caused her to faint. Why?

'Holly!' the writer's voice cut through her thoughts. 'We'd better be going.'

It was Belinda who first noticed something was wrong. 'Hold it!' she cried out as they approached the car. 'There's a flat tyre.'

Holly knelt down to examine it.

'This isn't an ordinary flat tyre,' she said. 'It's been cut with a knife. They've slashed it to ribbons.'

'This one too,' said Tracy. All four tyres had received the same treatment.

'Now what do we do?' moaned Belinda.

They looked to Benson for the decision. But the writer had frozen, her hand resting on the half open car door.

Holly took control. 'We'd best go back inside and report it to the police.'

Suddenly Benson came back to life. 'No. No police,' she insisted. 'Whoever did it will be long gone by now. I'll leave the car here overnight. I'll telephone for a couple of taxis. One for me and one for you three.'

'No need to get a taxi for us,' said Holly. 'I'll phone home. One of my parents will come and get us.'

'OK!' said Benson. 'Maybe that's best.'

Holly and Tracy left Belinda and Benson sitting in the reception area while they went off to make the phone calls. The writer appeared quite happy to let somebody else make the arrangements. The slashing of the tyres had left her badly shaken.

The phone number of a mini-cab firm was on a card inside the telephone box. Holly rang them and then dialled her home number. At the first attempt it was engaged. But the second time she got through. Her father answered the phone and didn't seem at all surprised to be called out to collect Holly. He was so easy-going since they'd moved away from London that nothing upset him anymore. Not even the Mystery Club's exploits.

When Holly and Tracy returned from the phone box they found Belinda sitting alone.

'Where is she?' Holly asked.

'Gone!' Belinda replied.

'Gone where?'

'In the taxi. It came a minute ago.'

'It couldn't possibly have done,' said Holly. 'I only just rang for it!'

'Well, all I know is a car drew up outside and hooted its horn,' said Belinda. 'Benson said she'd better not keep it waiting and to tell you she'd be in touch soon.'

'You sure it was a taxi?' Holly was anxious.

Belinda shrugged. 'Who else could it be?'

'Did you see it?'

'Not really. It's getting pretty dark out there. Why, what's wrong?'

'I wish I knew,' said Holly. 'I really wish I knew!'

12 Suspects

Holly, Tracy and Belinda were breathing hard as they reached the top of the hill. It had been a long bicycle ride. And in spite of doing most of it in easy gear, Belinda's legs felt as though they were about to give up.

'Greg's barbecue had better be worth it,' she panted. 'I could eat a horse after this ride.'

'That's probably not the best choice of words,' Tracy shouted over her shoulder as she began to freewheel down the hill towards Hanover Hall.

Holly laughed as she slipped in behind Tracy, her light brown hair flowing behind her in the breeze. This ride was just what she needed. Mr Adams had been out all day at a craft fair, so Holly had had to do the job she hated most – looking after Jamie. She had tried her best to keep well away from him.

For most of the day she'd read *Tomb Treasures of Ancient Egypt*. She was amazed and fascinated by the hundreds of different objects found inside the Pyramids and in the famous Valley of the Kings. Not only the mummies and sarcophagi, furniture and statues but smaller, everyday objects like combs, mirrors, jewellery, all made more than three thousand years ago.

She could see how people got hooked on the subject. In fact, she began to think that maybe she had found the right topic for her school project. But what she couldn't understand was why Crawford was interested in it. He seemed too selfish and self-centred to be interested in the subject for its own sake. Yet something clearly attracted him to it. But what?

She was getting nowhere. She decided to put it all right out of her mind. It was no good to keep going over the same things time and time again. Try as she might, though, her thoughts kept drifting back to the events of the previous night.

Her parents had listened politely as she told them how the taxi had turned up almost immediately. But neither of them was very surprised. 'I expect they already had somebody in the area,' her mother said. 'On the way back from another job. It often happens.'

Her father agreed. 'And another thing,' he pointed out. 'If it wasn't a genuine taxi, the real one would have turned up soon after.'

'Maybe it did,' said Holly. 'After you'd collected us. And then there's the slashed tyres. What about them?'

'Vandalism,' said Mrs Adams. 'Pure and simple.'

Mr Adams could see that Holly was not convinced. 'Look,' he said. 'You may not think it
very likely. But it's more likely to be vandalism
than kidnapping.'

Put that way Holly could see the weakness in her
case. There were perfectly good explanations for
what had happened. Yet she still felt that something
was wrong. And in the past her feelings had often
proved to be right.

But no matter how much she thought about it,
nothing was fitting into place. So it was something
of a relief to get out on the open road and forget
for a while.

The bikes raced down the hill, picking up speed
all the time. Tracy was in front, crouched low over
the handlebars to reduce wind resistance, then
Holly and finally Belinda bringing up the rear.

Holly braked slightly and sat tall in the saddle.
There was no rush. She might as well enjoy
the ride.

Over to the left the hill rose sharply towards a
small wood. Holly wondered if that was where
Belinda had first seen the man with the pony-tail.
Suddenly there was a glint of light from near the
edge of the wood. She tried to keep her eyes on
the spot. There it was again. And another a short
distance away.

'Hold it!' Holly shouted and slammed on her
brakes.

'Look out!' came a yell from behind. The next moment Belinda hurtled past, trying desperately to control her skidding back wheel. Holly watched in horror as Belinda careered across the road and disappeared into the hedge.

Holly jumped off her bike and raced over to the tangle of branches, wheels and legs that was Belinda. From the way she was yelling Holly guessed she wasn't too badly injured.

It was difficult to make out where the hedge ended and Belinda began. But a leg sticking out from the wreckage seemed to be largely free of complications. So Holly grabbed it and tugged. A very angry Belinda emerged.

'What was the idea suddenly braking like that?' she yelled. 'I could have broken my neck!'

'Sorry,' said Holly, picking bits of hedge out of Belinda's hair. 'I thought I saw something.'

'You what?' Belinda looked as though she were about to explode.

'Have you been trying to jump hedges again?' said Tracy, slightly breathless after pedalling back up the hill. 'You really ought to have realised by now, Belinda, horses jump hedges. Bikes don't.'

'You two will be jumping a hedge in a minute,' Belinda snarled. 'With my foot underneath you.'

'It was my fault,' Holly explained. She grabbed hold of Belinda's bike and heaved. With a snapping

124

of branches the hedge suddenly released it. Holly stumbled backwards.

'She just slammed on the brakes. Right in front of me. I hadn't got a chance,' Belinda complained.

'Any particular reason?' said Tracy, straightening the bike's handlebars.

'You bet,' said Holly. 'I saw flashing lights up there in the wood.'

'See? I knew it!' Belinda yelled triumphantly. Suddenly her aches and pains were forgotten. 'It's those men. They're still up there.'

'If they're still up there, where's the van?' said Tracy. 'It's not on the road. And anyway, why would they be messing around with lights in broad daylight?'

Holly was straining on tiptoe trying to see over the top of the hedge. 'I don't think it was lights. I think it was more like the sun reflecting on their binoculars.

'I told you, they're keeping watch on the stables,' said Belinda. 'Waiting for their chance to get to the Blushing Bride.'

'Where did you see them? Point it out,' said Tracy.

'We'll see better from back there,' Holly told them. Further up the road there was a break in the hedge where a gate led into the field. From there there was a clear view up the hill to the wood.

'You see where those bushes are just in front of

the trees?' said Holly as she climbed up the gate. 'It was to the right of them. But further in.'

Holly and Tracy peered up towards the wood, searching for any signs of life. But Belinda's attention had been grabbed by something else. She was looking down the hill. There, in a dip behind the hedge, out of sight from the road, was the red transit van.

With a whoop of delight, Belinda began clambering over the gate. 'Look what I've found!' she shouted as she dropped into the field and ran towards the van.

By the time Holly and Tracy reached her, Belinda was already peering in through the back window. 'The camping gear's gone,' she said.

'What is in there?'

'Coils of rope . . . helmets . . . spades . . . a couple of gas bottles . . . a petrol can. I can't make out everything.'

'Let me see,' said Tracy. 'My eyes are better than yours.'

But before Tracy could move, a distant voice shouted out, 'Hey, you lot! What do you think you're up to?'

Holly twisted round. The two men were racing down the hill towards them.

'They don't look too pleased with us,' said Tracy.

'Back to the bikes. Quick!' yelled Holly.

The men had some distance to cover but they were running downhill. They reached the gate just as the Mystery Club reached their bikes.

'Let's go!' shouted Holly.

They went, pedalling like mad and leaving the men shouting angrily after them. This time they didn't slow down until they reached the driveway to Hanover Hall.

Greg was waiting for them by the main gates.

'Is something wrong?' he said as they pulled up. 'You look hassled.'

'It's a long story,' said Belinda. 'We'll tell you about it while we eat. We are still going to eat?' she added anxiously.

'Of course, it's all set up. This way.' Greg strode off down a path that led towards the river. Holly, Tracy and Belinda followed on behind with their bikes.

'You're sure nobody minds us being here?' Holly asked.

'Not as long as you keep away from the stables,' said Greg striding ahead. He carried on for a few paces then stopped. 'Actually,' he said. 'Nobody knows. I was going to ask Mr Shah but after yesterday morning it didn't seem like a good idea.'

'Great!' Tracy snorted. 'It looks like we're going to get chased off here as well.'

'No. It's OK,' said Greg. 'There's nobody around.

Mr Shah is out, Hinkley is looking after the stables, and it's the housekeeper's night off. So nobody will know you've been. Especially where we're going. You can't see it from the house.' Greg turned and carried on towards the river.

It was a perfect spot for a barbecue. Right on the riverbank and sheltered by a circle of trees.

Greg had built the barbecue himself out of bricks and wire-mesh fencing. The coals were already white-hot, and before long they were all tucking into burgers, sausages and packets of crisps.

'So you think they're the ones who are out to nobble the Bride, do you?' Greg seemed amused by the story Belinda had just told.

'I'm certain of it,' Belinda had no doubt.

'I'm not so sure,' said Holly. She took out a handkerchief and started to wipe her hands.

'Come on then, Miss Marple,' said Tracy. 'Don't keep us in suspense.'

'I think it's Shah they're interested in.'

'Shah?'

'It was him they were following that day at the bank. What do you think, Greg?'

Greg thought about it for a moment. 'He's got plenty of enemies,' he said. 'He can be pretty ruthless in business.'

'He must have plenty of money too,' said Tracy. 'Maybe they're planning to rob him.'

Belinda almost choked in her excitement. 'What

about the things in the back of the van?' she sput-tered. 'They could be used to break in, couldn't they?'

'That's not exactly proof,' said Greg. 'I've got things in the boot of my car that *could* be used to break in, but that doesn't mean I'm a burglar. And Shah is hardly likely to have large sums of money hanging around the house.'

'He was at the bank,' Holly pointed out.

'Getting our wages,' said Greg. 'No, I'm sorry, girls, but I think you're getting a bit carried away. Things like this just don't happen in real life. Believe me.'

There was a long uncomfortable silence. The only noises were the crackling sounds of the hot charcoal and the ripple of the river in the reeds.

Greg was the first to break the silence. 'Anybody want another sausage?' he asked.

They all shook their heads.

Tracy stood up. 'I don't know about you guys,' she said. 'But I think it's time we were going. It's getting dark.'

'We better clean up first,' said Holly. 'Who's going to help wash up in the river?'

Belinda stumbled over towards the bikes. 'I'll get my lamp so we can see what we're doing.' she said. A moment later she let out a cry of despair. 'Oh no! It's gone. My lamp's gone. It must have come off when I crashed into the hedge.'

'Don't worry,' said Tracy. 'We'll look for it tomorrow.'

'That's not the point,' Belinda moaned. 'How am I going to get home without a light on my bike?'

Greg jumped to his feet. 'That's OK,' he said. 'I'll run you back in the wreck. It's parked over at the back of the stables. Lend me a bike and I'll go and fetch it.'

Ten minutes later Greg was back. He was still riding Tracy's bike and he had a face as long as a wet weekend. 'Forget the lift,' he moaned. 'Both my headlights have been smashed.'

'Smashed?' said Holly. 'Who'd do something like that?'

'I bet I know,' said Belinda.

'So do I,' said Greg. 'Hinkley. He blames me for getting him into trouble with Mr Shah. I told you he'd find a way of getting his own back.'

'But it was all his fault,' Belinda complained. 'You weren't to blame.'

'Things like that don't bother Hinkley. Look after number one is his motto. And he'll go to any lengths to do it.' Greg kicked a tuft of grass into the river. 'Well, I'm sorry but there's no way I can take you back now. Not without headlights.'

'Uh-oh. It looks like my dad's going to have to come to the rescue again,' said Holly.

'Do you think he will?' Belinda pleaded. 'My

mother's out at a Music Society rehearsal. And dad's in Amsterdam.'

'Only one problem,' said Holly. 'Where's the nearest phone?'

Greg offered Holly a key. 'Here,' he said. 'There's one up at the Hall. You and Belinda can use that while Tracy and I get things sorted out here.'

Holly turned the key in the lock. Greg had been certain that there'd be nobody up at the Hall. 'And anyway,' he'd told them, 'Mr Shah wouldn't mind you using the phone. Not in an emergency,' But Holly wasn't so sure.

The house was in darkness. Holly pushed the door open and felt for the light switch. She flicked it on.

The entrance hall was immense. It was bigger than Holly's lounge and dining-room put together. Straight ahead was a staircase you could have driven a tank up. To the right of the staircase there was a door leading to the rear of the house. There were other doors in the side walls leading into downstairs rooms.

'Wow!' said Belinda. 'Even my mother would find this a bit over the top. This hall is big enough to play tennis in.'

'Come on,' said Holly. 'We've got a phone call to make.'

The telephone was on a small, elegantly carved

131

table near the bottom of the stairs. It was an old model, the kind with a dial and a big heavy receiver. Holly and Belinda sat on the bottom step while Holly phoned home.

Mr and Mrs Adams were still having dinner so Holly arranged to be picked up by the main gates in an hour's time. 'Oh and by the way, Dad,' Holly had said finally, 'make sure the bike rack is fixed on because there are three bikes to bring back as well.' Holly replaced the receiver in its cradle and stood up.

'Let's get out of here,' she said, walking towards the front door.

'Do you think we should leave the money for the phone call?' Belinda said with a grin. The next moment the grin was wiped off her face as a car roared up the drive and screeched to a halt outside.

Belinda ran forward and grabbed hold of Holly's arm. 'There's somebody here!' she blurted out.

'It's OK,' said Holly. 'Greg said Mr Shah wouldn't mind us making a phone call.'

'Do you believe that?'

'No!'

Holly flicked off the hall light. She grabbed hold of Belinda and bundled her through one of the side doors. The room was in darkness but in one corner Holly could just make out the bulky outline of a huge sofa. 'Behind that!' she whispered.

They could already hear voices in the hallway. Angry voices, raised in argument. If there was still any doubt in their minds about whether to hide from the racehorse owner the sound of his shouting got rid of it. They dived behind the sofa.

At the same time the door opened and a light was switched on.

'Now look, Shah,' said a woman's voice. She had a strong Scottish accent. 'Shouting is going to get you nowhere. You'll just have to learn that you don't always get your own way.'

'We had a deal,' Shah said icily. 'And now you're trying to go back on it. Nobody does that to me!'

The woman laughed. 'If that's a threat I'd better tell you now, I don't scare easily.'

'Eighty thousand pounds, that's what we agreed. Eighty thousand. Payable on receipt of the goods.'

'Yes.' the woman agreed. 'But now someone else is interested. He may be willing to pay more. I'm just giving you the opportunity to increase your bid.'

'Who is it? Who else is in the bidding?'

'Someone who is willing to pay to get what he wants.'

'You're lying. There is no one else. This is just a bluff. Eighty thousand is my final offer.'

The woman's voice took on a new tone. 'Look, these are precious items. They'd be the greatest jewels of any collection. You won't get another chance to buy. They're rare. Very rare. Not only that but there's the risk involved. Half the customs officers in the world are on the lookout for them.'

'I thought you said they were already in Holland.'

'They are. But I still have to get them here, don't I? And if I'm risking my neck I want paying for it.'

There was a brief pause. When Shah replied it was with an icy coolness. 'I've told you. I don't get involved in auctions. Eighty thousand is my final offer. Accept it here and now or the deal is off.'

'It's not enough.'

'Then you'll have to do business with someone else. Get out.'

There was a note of panic in the woman's voice. 'Look – you're making a big mistake.'

'Just get out. Our dealings are over. I don't trust you.'

'You'll regret this, you know.' The woman spat out the words. 'There's a way of getting back at you that'll cost you a lot more than eighty thousand pounds.'

'What are you talking about?'

'You'll find out soon enough.'

'Just go. Now!'

The woman was breathing heavily trying hard to control her anger. 'The least you can do is phone a taxi for me.'

'No. I don't want anyone to know that you've been here. I'll drop you off.' Shah's footsteps crossed the room. 'And after that I never want to see you again. Do you understand?' The light went off and the front door slammed.

Behind the sofa, Belinda and Holly waited for the sound of the car to disappear into the distance before speaking.

'What was all that about then?' said Belinda.

'I don't know,' said Holly. 'But let's get out of here before he comes back! There's more to Mr Shah than meets the eye. And if he knew we'd overheard all that, we might just find ourselves in a whole lot of trouble!'

13   Listening in

'But who was this woman?'

'We couldn't see. And Shah never mentioned her name so there's no way of knowing. I'd recognise her voice again though.'

The members of the Mystery Club were sitting by the fountain in the Willow Dale Shopping Centre. They were waiting for Steve Biggins and Jeff Padman to show up. Jeff was a friend from school who was working at Holly's mother's bank over the break.

It was something of a red-letter day for Willow Dale. Members of a number-one pop group were making a personal appearance at the shopping centre's record store. It was part of a promotional tour to sell their latest album. The Mystery Club had arranged to go along with Steve and Jeff.

In the meantime they were trying to make some sense out of the argument between Shah and the woman.

'Whatever it was, it was against the law,' said Belinda.

'And it involved smuggling something into the country. From Holland,' Holly added. 'Something customs officers would want to get their hands on.'

'Jewels. That's what she said.' Belinda reminded her. 'Rare and precious jewels. Diamonds most probably. Eighty thousand pounds worth.'

Tracy stood up. 'I don't like it,' she said. 'It's a little like Belinda's hair.'

'What do you mean?'

'There are too many loose ends!'

'Hysterical!' said Belinda scornfully. 'I hope you're a better detective than you are a comedian.'

Holly ignored the bickering. 'I know what you mean,' she said. 'It's like trying to do a jigsaw without some of the pieces that make it fit together.'

'Don't panic,' said Belinda confidently. 'Nothing defeats the Mystery Club. Sooner or later something is bound to turn up.'

'It already has,' said Tracy, waving across the concourse. 'Here's Steve.'

Steve Biggins nodded a greeting.

'Anything to report from the health club, Steve?' Tracy asked.

'Nothing,' Steve replied. 'I've been keeping a close eye on things. But Crawford's been particularly low-key the last couple of days. He's keeping himself to himself.'

'That's a shame,' said Tracy. 'We need something else to happen.'

'Why not come over tonight then?' Steve suggested. 'The boss is away for the night, so I'm in charge. There'll be no problem getting you all in. And things always seem to happen when you're around.'

'You're on,' said Holly. 'Now what's happened to Jeff? He said he'd be here ten minutes ago.'

'Let's give him another five minutes,' said Belinda.

Jeff arrived just as they were about to leave. He was clearly flustered and a bit on edge. 'I'm really sorry,' he apologised. 'Trouble with a customer.'

'Not a bank robbery?' Holly said with a grin.

'That might have been easier. Some woman wanted to take out a large amount of money. In five pound notes. I was given the job of checking with her bank.'

'What's so difficult about that?'

'They were a bit worried. It was a lot of money to take out in cash. They thought maybe the cheque book had been stolen. So they asked for a description of the woman. But when I told them what she looked like, they said it wasn't her.'

Holly stepped on to the escalator that led to the upper level. 'So she had stolen the cheque book then?'

'No. That was the embarrassing thing. The assistant manager had her in his office for a little while. Then he said to give her the money. Believe me, she wasn't too pleased about it all.'

Holly was about to ask more about the woman when Tracy shouted from the top of the escalator. She was pointing down into the shopping centre below. There, hurrying towards the exit that led to the multi-storey carpark was P.J. Benson. She was carrying a small black suitcase.

Holly and Tracy watched as Benson disappeared through the carpark doors.

Jeff was waiting with a puzzled look on his face.

'It's all right,' Holly explained. 'We just saw somebody we knew.' Jeff's face didn't change. Something was bothering him. Suddenly Holly realised what it was. 'That was her, wasn't it?' she said. 'That was the woman in the bank?'

Jeff said nothing. But his eyes told Holly that her guess was spot-on.

'There must be a simple explanation.'

Holly and Tracy were in the Paradise juice bar after their workout. Belinda had decided that the last thing she needed after a day at the stable was more exercise, so Holly and Tracy were going to visit her later. In the meantime they were busy discussing Benson.

'Maybe she was just transferring money from

139

one bank to another,' said Holly. She desperately wanted to find a reasonable explanation for the writer's behaviour.

'If she wanted to do that,' Tracy pointed out, 'she didn't have to get cash. She could just have written a cheque. No, she was drawing money out. Large amounts of it.'

Holly knew that Tracy had to be right. 'But why?' she said. 'Why would she want so much cash?'

'Add it to the list of mysteries,' said Tracy.

At that moment Steve Biggins appeared behind the reception desk. He waved to Tracy and Holly and motioned them into the office.

'Have I got news for you!' he announced dramatically as he closed the door. 'I know why Crawford's been behaving so strangely.'

'Don't tell us. He's an escaped convict!' said Tracy.

Steve shook his head. 'Nothing so unusual,' he said. 'He's been seeing a woman.'

'And that's enough to make him use a different name, knock me off my bike, steal my camera and ruin my film?' Tracy's voice was heavy with sarcasm.

'It is if he doesn't want anybody to know about it. If he's desperate to keep it secret.'

'Why would he want to keep it so secret?'

'Do I have to spell it out? Maybe he's already married. Or he's got more than one girlfriend. Or his mother doesn't think he's old enough to go out with girls! I don't know the reason. I'm just telling you what's been going on.' Steve was beginning to lose his temper.

'I'm sure you're right, Steve.' Holly tried to cool things down. 'But how did you find out?'

Steve explained how earlier that evening a woman had phoned and asked to speak to Crawford. Steve had fetched him from the swimming pool. But rather than walk all the way back to his room Crawford had said he'd take the call in the office.

'And you listened in,' Tracy guessed.

'I couldn't avoid hearing,' Steve protested. 'He was so mad. Yelling about what did she think she was doing phoning him here. And that he didn't want to meet her again in case anybody saw them. And that if anything ever came out in public he'd say they'd never even met.'

'Is that all?'

'No. He went quiet for a bit then. I couldn't hear so well. But I think he said if she'd got anything to tell him she'd have to do it through someone else. Then he slammed the phone down on her.'

For a moment no one spoke. Tracy looked as though she'd just found out there was no Father Christmas. Sadly she shook her head. 'You know, Holly,' she sighed, 'I've got a horrible feeling another mystery has just bitten the dust!'

*　　*　　*

Belinda was saying goodnight to Meltdown when Holly and Tracy arrived. Her face lit up. 'Just wait till you hear what I've got to tell you!' she cried.

Tracy stopped her dead. 'Whatever it is, it's nothing compared to our news. Listen to this.'

Between them Holly and Tracy told Belinda everything that Steve Biggins had said. If they expected her to be surprised they were sadly disappointed. As they finished she gave a mocking laugh.

'I never thought there was much of a mystery there in the first place,' she said. 'I've been trying to get you to understand. It's the men in the van who need watching. Now do you want to hear my news or not?'

Belinda explained she had cycled over to Hanover Hall to look for her bike lamp. After a little while she'd found it. In the long grass near the base of the hedge. Luckily it still worked.

'And that's your exciting news?' Tracy exclaimed.

'Of course not! I was just putting the lamp back on the bracket when I heard voices coming from behind the hedge on the other side of the road.'

Holly and Tracy sat up and took notice.

'At first they were too far away for me to tell what they were saying. But as they got nearer I began to make it out.'

'What did they say?'

Belinda paused for a moment, trying to get it clear

142

in her mind. 'One said, "We need somebody on the inside. Somebody who'll help us out." Then the other said, "That's got to be Hinkley. The news in town is that he's up to his neck in debt. He'll do anything for money. And there's no love lost between him and Shah these days."' Belinda paused.

'Is that it then?' said Tracy.

'No. I was just leaving a dramatic pause,' Belinda grinned. 'Then the other one said, "The sooner you meet up the better then. Tell Hinkley there's money in it for him. And nobody need ever know he was involved." Then the van door opened and the engine started up. So I decided I'd better make myself scarce.' Belinda looked triumphantly from Holly to Tracy and back again. 'Well?' she said proudly. 'What do you think?'

'I think things are beginning to fall into place,' said Holly.

14 The wrong track?

'Come on through to the kitchen,' said Tracy when Holly knocked on the door early the next afternoon. 'I've cooked us lunch.'

Holly was amazed. 'Since when were you into cooking?'

'I'm not,' Tracy replied. She placed two flat packets on the table, ripped open the tops, placed them in the microwave and switched on. 'There we are,' she said. 'Don't say I never do anything for you.'

It wasn't the best or the healthiest lunch Holly had ever had. But she had to admit one thing – it was certainly hot.

Tracy threw the empty packets into the rubbish bin. 'Keep your spoon,' she said. 'You'll need it for dessert.'

Dessert was the remains of a carton of toffee crunch ice-cream eaten direct from the plastic tub. Five minutes later, the plastic tub followed the microwave packets into the bin. The forks and spoons were rinsed under the tap and lunch was over.

'Thanks a lot,' said Holly, taking a swig of cola from the bottle. 'But there was no need to go to all that trouble.'

'Think nothing of it,' said Tracy. 'Now let's get down to business.'

Holly took out the Mystery Club's red notebook and prepared to take notes. 'Where do we start?'

'The Blushing Bride,' said Tracy. 'I hate to say it but it looks like Belinda was right. Those guys in the van are planning to get to Hinkley. And there's nobody in a better position to nobble the horse than he is.'

'They never actually said that's what they wanted him to do.'

'Well, what else could it be?'

Holly shrugged. 'Beats me.'

Tracy was certain. 'So that must be it.'

'In which case we need a plan to catch them out.'

'We need Belinda for that,' said Tracy. 'Inside information!'

'Agreed.' Holly flicked the pages of the notebook. 'Now, what about Mr Shah?'

Tracy held up her hands in mock surrender. 'That's down to you. What do you think?'

Holly chewed the end of her pen. 'I think we're stuck. Whatever it was he was up to he's pulled out now. That just leaves us with a nameless, faceless woman with a Scottish accent who might be smuggling something into the country. Not much to go on.'

Tracy pulled a face. 'I guess not even the Mystery Club can do much about that.'

'Nor about Benson,' said Holly. 'All I can think of there is blackmail.'

'It would explain the suitcase full of cash,' Tracy agreed. 'But who would blackmail her? And why?'

'Thinking it through,' said Holly, 'what have we got?'

'Her acting weird – all the secrecy,' said Tracy.

'That could just be because she wants to avoid publicity.'

'Or because she's got something to hide.'

'But she's a famous writer,' Holly protested.

'So she's got more to lose,' Tracy insisted. 'Check back. Maybe we've missed something. What was it that freaked her out when she was doing that interview?'

Holly thought about it. 'It seemed to be when Ainsley James mentioned some woman called McLean. He said she was a friend of Benson's brother. Not much of a reason to get upset, is it?'

'That's what makes it suspicious,' said Tracy. 'I think there's more to this brother business than meets the eye. What else have we got?'

Holly looked through her notes. 'The dark blue

146

car. It was there outside the park. And it followed us from the church to the restaurant.'

'Right.'

'*If* it was the same one,' Holly pointed out. 'There are lots of cars that colour around – Greg's, for one.'

Tracy pounced on this. 'Exactly. And look how Benson reacted when she saw that.'

Holly had to admit that Tracy was right. The blue car had to be involved somehow. But how? And who was the woman Holly had seen driving it?

Her thoughts were interrupted by the telephone.

'Typical!' said Tracy going out to answer it. 'Just when we were starting to get somewhere.'

When Tracy came back from taking the phone call she was flushed with excitement. 'That was Steve.' She grabbed her coat. 'He says to get to the health club right away. Something's going on.'

'What?'

'He couldn't say on the phone. Come on!'

Steve Biggins was washing down the big glass doors that formed the entrance to Paradise. 'I thought you were never going to get here,' he said. 'It's the third time I've cleaned these. People are getting suspicious.'

'Is that what you called us over for?' said Tracy. 'To admire your handiwork?'

'Don't be ridiculous.' Steve threw the wash

147

leather into the bucket. The water splashed over the rim on to the floor. Nervously he checked round to make sure no one else could hear. 'It's Crawford. There's a guy here come to interview him.'

'A detective?' asked Tracy.

'No. Not a detective,' Steve was irritated. 'Of course, not a detective. Don't you ever think of anything else? Somebody's come to do an interview with him. He's famous.'

Tracy was bewildered. 'How can he be famous? I've never heard of him.'

'Crawford's not his real name, is it? I sneaked a look in his file after the interviewer turned up. He's using a false identity.'

Tracy clapped her hands with excitement. 'I knew it!'

'What is his real name then?' asked Holly.

Steve dropped his voice. 'Crawford's real name is Michael John Barratt.'

'Barratt?' Tracy shook her head. 'Michael John?'

'Mike!' said Steve. 'Mean anything?'

'Mike Barratt,' yelled Holly. 'The film actor?'

'Star, I would have called him,' said Steve. 'The film star. He's here to get in shape for his next picture.'

'Is this some sort of joke?' said Tracy. 'That guy is short, fat, bald and wears glasses. How can he be Mike Barratt?'

'Ever heard of wigs and make-up?' said Steve.

'Now take my advice. No matter how unpleasant he is, that guy is important. So lay off him. My job could be on the line here.' He picked up the bucket and turned to go back into the club. But as he did so the door opened and Ainsley James stepped out.

Holly's mouth opened in surprise.

James looked down at the water that had splashed on to the floor. 'I am so sorry,' he apologised. 'Did I make you spill that?'

'No, no, it's OK,' mumbled Steve.

'No, really, it was very clumsy of me.' James's eyes flicked from Steve to Tracy and finally came to rest on Holly. 'Just a minute,' he said. 'It's Holly, isn't it?'

Holly tried to smile.

'What are you doing here?' For the first time the reporter seemed to be rattled.

'Oh, just sort of visiting,' Holly replied. 'My friend here is a member.'

Ainsley James glanced at Tracy and nodded. 'Well, enjoy yourself,' he said. He started to move away.

Holly tried desperately to gather her thoughts together. 'What are you doing here?' she blurted out. 'Interviewing somebody?'

James stopped and turned back to look at Holly. For a moment he hesitated, as if he were unsure how to respond. 'As a matter of fact I am.'

'Anybody famous?'

The reporter switched on the smile. 'Nobody you'd know,' he said. 'Now I've got to rush. I've got a deadline to meet.'

Holly and Tracy called at Belinda's on the way back from Paradise. But there was no one there.

'Maybe she's found out that the Blushing Bride is really a film star called Black Beauty,' said Tracy, 'and she's rushed off to the police.'

'I'll phone her later,' grinned Holly. 'And tell her we've solved the Crawford mystery. Or should I say the Mike Barratt mystery?'

'Well, I'll always think of him as the Water Buffalo,' Tracy said.

When Holly arrived home her father was looking worried.

'What's wrong?' said Holly.

'It's your mother. The police phoned half an hour ago and asked her to go back to the bank.'

Holly's hopes began to rise. 'Not a robbery, is it?'

Mr Adams' face relaxed into a smile. 'Nothing so dramatic. They're after information.'

Holly put her arm around her father's waist. 'So as long as Mum's not been stashing money away into a secret Swiss bank account everything should be OK. You sit down and watch telly while I make us something to eat.'

Halfway through their meal the phone rang.

'That's probably your mother now,' said Mr Adams. But before he could move Jamie had shot off to answer it. A few seconds later he was back.

'It's for you,' he said to Holly. 'It's Belinda the wonder horse!'

Now it was Holly's turn to race to the phone. 'Hi! Have I got something to tell you,' she said into the receiver.

'Whatever it is, forget it.'

Even on the phone Holly could tell that Belinda was excited.

'I've got news which will blow you out of your seat,' said Belinda.

'I'm not in a seat,' said Holly.

'Then you'd better sit down. You'll need to.'

'Why? What's the news?'

'They've arrested Hinkley. He was caught trying to dope the Blushing Bride.'

Holly sat down with a bump.

'Well,' said Belinda triumphantly. 'What do you think of that?'

The story as Belinda told it was quite simple. She had gone over to Hanover Hall late that morning to find a police car parked in the stable yard. Greg and Mr Shah were being questioned by detectives.

During the previous night, Greg had been unable to sleep. So he'd gone down to the stables to fetch a book that he'd left there. As he'd entered, Hinkley had been about to give the racehorse an injection. He'd taken one look at Greg and dropped the syringe. Then he'd made a break for the door and raced off into the night.

The syringe contained a drug which would have given the horse all the symptoms of equine flu. Once that had been diagnosed she would never have been allowed to run in the big race.

As for Hinkley, the police had picked him up later trying to hitch a lift on the main road south. He was currently helping the police with their enquiries.

When Holly repeated the story to her father, he listened with growing amazement. 'How do you girls do it?' he said. 'You seem to attract mysteries like a magnet.'

'That's not all,' said Holly with a smile. 'We know who put Hinkley up to it.'

Mr Adams' brow creased into a frown as Holly told him about the men in the red van.

'I don't know whether that actually proves anything,' he said when she had finished. 'But I think tomorrow the three of you ought to go along to the police station and tell them all you know.'

It was almost eleven o'clock when Mrs Adams arrived home. As soon as she walked in it was clear that something was wrong. Her face was tense and worried.

Holly went straight out to the kitchen to make tea.

From there she could hear her parents talking in low voices. By the time the tea was made, her mother had taken off her coat and was sitting on the sofa. She motioned for Holly to sit next to her.

'What's the matter?' Holly could sense that something unusual was going on. 'What did the police want?'

'They wanted me to help trace some money that they think may have been used in a crime.'

'What sort of crime?'

'Well, you seem to have found out about it already,' Mrs Adams said. 'It was this attempt to dope the racehorse.'

'Tell me about it.' Holly sensed it was something important.

'Well, the man they've arrested—'

'Hinkley.'

'Hinkley. Yes. Well, he was carrying quite a lot of money. New notes, still in serial number order. They asked all the banks to check if they could find who the money had been issued to.'

Holly was ahead of the story. 'Because he'd been paid to do it. And the money would lead them to the people behind it all.'

'That's right.'

'And did the money come from your bank?'

Holly's mother nodded. 'It did.'

'And were you able to track down who it was paid to?'

'Eventually.'

Holly was beside herself with excitement. It just had to be the men in the van. 'Who was it?'

Mrs Adams paused before answering. 'Well, I shouldn't really tell you. But it'll be all over the news by the morning. The money was paid over to a woman. A woman by the name of Benson.'

Holly began to feel faint.

'Benson?' she echoed.

'P.J. Benson.'

Holly felt as though she were in a dream. 'It can't be,' she muttered. 'There must be some mistake.'

'I don't think so, Holly. The police are arresting P.J. Benson for being an accessory to the attempted doping of the Blushing Bride!'

15 Guilty as charged

It was the early hours of the morning before Holly finally fell asleep. The news of Benson's arrest had left her in a state of shock. Benson *couldn't* have been behind the attempted doping. Holly was certain of that. But if she wasn't, how had her money ended up with Hinkley? That was the puzzle. There had to be an answer to it. But Holly couldn't work it out.

The alarm was set for seven o'clock. Holly decided to phone Tracy and Belinda early. She had to let them know what had happened before they heard it on the news. But for once she slept right through. When she opened her eyes she saw that it was eight fifteen.

Holly jumped out of bed and pulled on her dressing-gown. Minutes later she was dialling Tracy's number. Tracy's mother answered the phone.

'Sorry,' she said in reply to Holly's enquiry, 'but Tracy went out about half an hour ago. She's gone over to Paradise to use the pool before it gets busy. Can I give her a message?'

'No, it's OK, Mrs Foster. I'll catch up with her later.'

Holly briefly replaced the receiver then started to dial Belinda's number.

It was a bright sunny day and Tracy was looking forward to her morning swim. She pedalled effortlessly along the country road that led to Paradise. Tracy enjoyed cycling on her own. It gave her time to relax. She put her brain into neutral and just let her thoughts roam.

Suddenly she was jolted out of her daydream by the sight of a dark blue car parked a couple of hundred metres ahead. It was pulled over on to the rough grass verge which separated the roadway from a thick belt of trees.

As far as Tracy could see, there was no one in the car. She brought her bike to a stop and jumped off. There must have been hundreds of similar cars in the area. But even as she walked towards it Tracy knew what she was going to find.

She stepped on to the grass and looked along the side. The passenger door mirror was missing. It had broken off. She was looking at the car that had knocked her off her bike. The same car that had picked up Crawford – Mike Barratt – that night.

She checked around. There was no sign of the driver. She felt the bonnet. It was still warm. The car hadn't been parked long.

Tracy grabbed her bicycle and rode thirty or forty metres down the road. She hid the bike in a clump of bushes. Then she set off through the trees in search of the driver.

The woman wasn't hard to spot. Within a few minutes Tracy had her in sight.

That's got to be her, Tracy thought. *The woman Mike Barratt's been seeing on the sly, But what's she doing here? That's supposed to be all over.*

The woman was tall with shoulder-length fair hair and was wearing a white raincoat. She was standing just inside the trees, looking across the field towards the health club.

Tracy followed her gaze. A single figure was toiling its way round the jogging track. Even from that distance Tracy knew who it was. The film star was still trying to lose weight!

Slowly he plodded round towards the spot where the woman was waiting. He seemed to have no idea she was there. When he was about fifty metres away the woman stepped forward on to the field and began to wave. Mike Barratt jogged on, head down, seeing nothing but the ground in front of him.

Tracy took her chance. Crouching low she crept forward as close as she dared to the spot where the woman was standing. A fallen tree, heavily draped with ivy, blocked her way. Tracy dropped to the ground and pulled herself into the space beneath the trunk. She reached out and gently parted the ivy that was blocking her view. The jogger was still heading towards the woman, unaware that there was anyone else around.

Suddenly, something made him look up. He stopped dead in his tracks. Then making sure that nobody else was watching he hurried forward and grabbed hold of the woman's arm. The next moment he was dragging her into the cover of the trees.

'What the hell are you doing here, McLean?' The name hit Tracy like a bomb. 'I told you not to come near here, didn't I? What if somebody sees us?' Barratt was very angry.

He looked out across the field then pulled the woman further into the woods. They stopped just a couple of metres away from the fallen tree. Tracy tried to pull herself even further underneath.

'Let go of my arm,' said the woman threateningly. She spoke with a Scottish accent. 'I had to come. There's been a change of plan.'

Barratt was alarmed. 'What's gone wrong?'

'Nothing for you to worry about. Just a little problem with one of my other projects. It's best that I get out of the area straight away.'

'If the police are on to you then it's all off.' There was panic in the man's voice.

'They're not. And by the time they are I'll be long gone. Now sit down and listen.'

The tree sagged as Mike Barratt lowered his weight on to it. Tracy could feel the pressure of the trunk against her chest. If the branches that were keeping it off the floor gave way then she would be crushed. She closed her eyes and tried to breathe deeply and silently.

'I'm on my way to Holland to pick up the goods now. I'm catching the twelve o'clock ferry. If everything goes smoothly – and it will – I'll be back tomorrow. You will meet me at three o'clock at Dock View Wharf. With the money. Got that?'

'Dock View Wharf? How do I find it?'

'Here's a map. Be there.'

'I will be.'

The tree lifted as the man stood up again. Tracy heard footsteps scuffling through the undergrowth. Through the gap in the ivy she saw Barratt begin to jog back across the field. A few minutes later a car engine started up and pulled away. Twisting around she rolled out of her hiding-place and sat up. She was ecstatic. The pieces were beginning to fit together. This wasn't about an affair. It was about smuggling! And Barratt was in it up to his neck. And the McLean woman was tied in with both Shah and Benson.

Tracy jumped on to her bike and headed back towards town as fast as she could. A kilometre or so along the road she met Holly coming in the opposite direction.

Before Tracy could say anything, Holly blurted out the news of Benson's arrest.

Tracy held out her arm. 'Pinch me,' she said. 'This is getting to be like a dream.'

'No time for that,' said Holly. She turned her bike round and set off back towards Willow Dale. 'We're meeting Belinda outside the police station in half an hour.'

'It's not actually proof,' said the sergeant at the desk.

'What do you want, their fingerprints on the syringe?' snapped Tracy. She was beginning to lose patience.

The police sergeant had been very polite and listened to Belinda's story about the men in the van. He had nodded encouragingly several times. He had even pursed his lips when she told him what they had said about Hinkley. But at the end of the story he was still unconvinced.

'Perhaps you didn't hear correctly. You were some distance away after all,' he said.

'I heard all right,' Belinda replied firmly. '"We need somebody on the inside," they said. '"Somebody who'll help us out." Then the other one said, "That's got to be Hinkley."'

'So it has to be them that bribed him. Not Benson,' Holly pointed out.

'Only problem with that is Hinkley was found

160

with Miss Benson's money on him,' said the police sergeant. 'How do you explain that?'

'There's a thousand reasons,' said Tracy, unable to think of a single one.

Belinda came to the rescue. 'Benson lost the money. The men in the van found it. And gave it to Hinkley.' Even she could see that it sounded unlikely.

The sergeant shook his head. 'If that's what happened, why doesn't Miss Benson tell us she lost it?'

'She doesn't have to prove she's innocent. You have to prove she's guilty!' said Belinda.

The policeman held up his hand. 'All right, I don't need any lectures on law from you, thank you, young lady.'

'She doesn't mean to be rude,' said Holly. 'It's just that we're certain that Benson is innocent and those men are guilty.'

'One hundred per cent guilty,' added Belinda.

The sergeant put down his pen and sighed. 'Look,' he said after a moment's thought. 'If I go and tell the officer in charge all this will you promise to go away?'

'It's a deal,' said Tracy.

The sergeant pointed towards a row of seats against the wall. 'Sit over there, please,' he said.

Holly, Tracy and Belinda sat on the chairs and the sergeant disappeared into a sideroom.

'I don't think I can stand the suspense,' said Holly anxiously.

'Fingers crossed,' said Belinda.

They didn't have to wait long. Within a few minutes the sergeant was back. He looked uncomfortable. 'The investigating officer says thank you very much for the information. He's taken note of it and won't need to detain you any longer.'

'Does that mean you're going to release Benson?' asked Tracy.

'Our enquiries into Miss Benson's activities will be continuing.'

'So you're not going to arrest those men? In spite of what I heard,' Belinda was getting angry now.

The policeman was trying hard not to lose patience. 'Look, I know it all seems straightforward to you. But you must realise it's not as simple as you think. We know what we're doing. We really do. And we appreciate your efforts. But—'

'Go away now!' Tracy completed his sentence.

'If that's the way you want to put it. Yes.'

Belinda started to make a long complaint but Tracy stopped her.

'You're wasting your time,' she said. She pulled Belinda towards the door. But Holly stayed where she was.

'Are we allowed to see Miss Benson, then?' she asked as calmly as she could.

The sergeant looked doubtful. 'Miss Benson is still being questioned, I'm afraid.'

But just then the door to the interview room opened and Benson was led out by a young policewoman. Benson came to a halt a couple of metres away from Holly. Her face was deathly pale and there were heavy lines round her eyes. She looked to be on the point of exhaustion. For a moment she stared silently at Holly, then past her to Belinda and Tracy. 'What are you doing here?' she asked.

'This way please, Miss Benson.' The policewoman was trying to move her along.

Holly turned to the desk sergeant. 'Can we?' she asked.

The sergeant waved the policewoman away. 'Just a couple of minutes,' he said. He walked back behind the desk and began shuffling through papers.

The Mystery Club crowded round Benson, all talking at once.

'Wait! Wait!' the writer said. 'I appreciate you coming to see me. But really I think you'd better go. There's nothing you can do.'

'But we know you're innocent,' Holly protested. 'And we intend to prove it.'

Benson closed her eyes and slowly shook her head. 'Please. Leave it,' she sighed. 'I know you only want to help. But really it'll be better if you leave things alone.'

'I don't understand,' said Holly. 'Are you saying you're guilty?'

'No!' said the writer. 'I'm not saying that. I'm just saying . . . I don't know what I'm saying. But please don't make matters worse than they are.' There were tears in Benson's eyes now and she looked as though she was about to lose control.

'Come along now, please, Miss Benson.' The policewoman took her by the arm and tried to lead her away.

The writer began to move with her then hesitated. 'Thank you,' she said, taking Holly by the hand. 'You don't know how much your concern means to me.'

And with that she was led away down to the cells.

16 Caught?

'Then if the police won't do anything about them we'll have to.'

The members of the Mystery Club were soaking up the morning sunshine outside the Blushing Bride's stable. There was no one else around. Greg was out exercising the racehorse, and Shah was away trying to find someone to take over from Hinkley.

'Well,' said Belinda, 'are we going to do anything or not?'

Holly closed her eyes and lifted her face to the sun. 'I'm thinking,' she said. 'Trying to work out the connections. This McLean woman seems to turn up everywhere. Following Benson. Meeting Shah. Meeting Mike Barratt. There has to be some sort of link. But what?'

'Not again,' said Belinda. She covered her face with her hands and moaned. 'Please not again.'

They had gone over the facts time and time again. But they were still left with unanswered questions.

'McLean has to be the same woman that was talking to Shah,' said Tracy. 'That part fits. She told him there was somebody else who was willing to pay big money. That's Mike Barratt. And the deal's happening this afternoon.'

'And there's nothing we can do about it,' said Belinda.

'Except go back to the police,' said Holly.

'Are you kidding?' Tracy couldn't believe her ears. 'What notice are they going to take? We practically hand them those guys up there on a plate, and they do nothing about it!'

'Which is why we have to do it ourselves,' Belinda insisted. 'It's the only way we're going to get Benson out of jail. And that's the most important thing.'

Tracy jumped to her feet. 'OK, Belinda,' she said. 'What do you suggest we do?'

'Go up there and search their camp. See if we can find anything that proves they put Hinkley up to it.'

'Oh, yes? And what are they going to be doing while we're doing that?'

Belinda dropped her bombshell. 'They're going to be protecting their van from vandals.'

There was silence for a moment. Holly and Tracy gazed suspiciously at Belinda, then turned to each other.

'I think she's got a plan,' Holly suggested.

Belinda's plan was simple. One of them would climb into the field and start to snoop around the van. The men would see her and run down the hill to stop her. At the last minute she would jump back over the gate and get away on her bike. While the men were away from their camp, the other two would search the tents.

'It's *too* simple,' said Tracy. 'It won't work.'

'It's the only plan we've got,' Holly pointed out. 'And it's better than doing nothing.'

Tracy thought for a while. 'OK!' she said. 'We'll do it. On one condition. Belinda snoops around the van.'

Belinda opened her mouth to protest, then stopped. It was her plan. She had to take the biggest risk.

By eleven o'clock Tracy and Holly were hiding up in the wood. Ahead of them was a small clearing. In the middle of this stood a large frame tent in army camouflage colours. On either side were two smaller bivouac tents. And towards the edge of the wood was a canvas bird-watchers' hide that looked out over the valley.

The men's voices seemed to be coming from the hide. Holly glanced anxiously at her watch. It was almost five past eleven. Belinda should have been in action by now. Perhaps something had gone wrong. Or perhaps it was just that the two men were too busy talking to notice her.

Suddenly angry shouts rang out. Seconds later, the two men raced out of the hide, crashed through the trees and headed off across the field.

'Let's go!' said Holly.

Within seconds they were entering the main tent. Holly headed straight for a small table covered in papers. Tracy began fumbling inside a large haversack.

Almost immediately a portable phone began to ring.

Tracy stopped searching. Holly looked up in alarm.

'Find it and stop it,' she said. 'Before they hear it.'

But that was easier said than done.

The noise was slightly muffled but seemed to be coming from the front corner of the tent. In that corner there was a chair with an anorak draped across the back, what looked like a pile of dirty clothes and a suitcase.

'Try the suitcase!' said Holly.

Tracy dived into the corner and started tugging at the zip.

Still the phone rang out.

Tracy flipped open the lid. The case was almost empty.

'Nothing!' she said.

'The clothes then.'

'I really don't think they'll fit you,' said an angry voice from the doorway. There, blocking the only way out of the tent, stood the man with the grey pony-tail.

He grabbed the anorak from the back of the chair, unzipped a pocket and took out the portable phone. 'This what you're looking for?' He pressed a button and spoke into the mouthpiece.

'Hello.'

There was a long pause as he listened.

'You're sure he's gone? He's not just trying to fool us?'

There was a second pause. Much shorter.

'OK,' he said. 'Thanks for letting us know.'

He closed the phone and put it back in the pocket of the anorak. All the time he kept his eyes firmly fixed on Holly and Tracy.

'Now what do you think you're up to?' he said at last.

Tracy tried to play innocent.

'We were just walking through the woods. We saw the tents. Thought we'd have a look inside.'

The man raised his eyebrows in wonder. 'Is that so?' he said, his voice heavy with sarcasm. 'And I suppose the other day you and that friend of yours just happened to find our van.'

'That's right.'

'I may be stupid. But I'm not that stupid.'

Holly tried a different tack.

'I don't know what you're planning to do with us,' she said. 'But I'd better warn you. That friend of ours is on her way to Hanover Hall right now. If we don't meet her there in ten minutes, she'll be phoning the police.'

'I don't think so.' From outside the tent a second voice spoke.

The man with the pony-tail looked round.

'Well, well, what have we got here?'

A very unhappy Belinda stumbled forward. Her jeans were ripped at the knee and there was a nasty red graze on her forehead.

Holly and Tracy rushed towards her.

'What have you done to her, you moron?' Tracy yelled.

'Who me?' said the man with the moustache. 'I never touched her!'

'I slipped and banged my head on the gate,' said Belinda. Her face reddened with the shame. 'That's why he caught me.'

Holly put her arm round Belinda. 'It's all right,' she whispered. 'We made a mess of it as well.'

The two men were standing side by side in the entrance to the tent looking at the girls.

'What are we going to do with them, Pete?' said the one with the moustache.

The other shook his head. 'I don't know, Phil. They won't say what they were up to.'

170

Phil took a step forward. 'What is it, eh? What is this all about?' He grabbed hold of Holly's wrist. 'C'mon, I want to know.'

Holly gasped, more with surprise than pain.

'It's not what we're up to,' she said. 'It's you. What you're up to. And we know all about it.'

The two men looked at each other. If they knew what Holly was talking about, they were giving nothing away.

'What do you know?' said Phil. He let go of Holly's wrist.

'We know it was you that got Hinkley to dope the Blushing Bride.'

Phil and Pete looked mystified.

'You know that, do you?' said Pete.

'Yes. And so do the police.'

'That's right.'

'Interesting. We *are* the police.'

It was the Mystery Club's turn to look mystified.

Tracy was the first to recover from the shock. 'Prove it,' she said.

Pete reached into the pocket of the anorak and took out a wallet. He opened it and showed Tracy his identification.

'I guess we got it wrong,' she said sheepishly. 'Oops!'

'I guess you did,' Phil told her. 'And it's lucky for you that we are the police. Because otherwise you could have been in serious trouble. Now what's all this about?'

Holly tried to explain. 'We saw you up here. We thought you were keeping watch on Hanover Hall. Waiting for your chance to get at the Blushing Bride.'

Belinda took over. 'Then the other day I heard you talking about Hinkley. Saying you needed inside help. And how he needed the money.'

'So when he was caught,' Holly continued, 'we thought you must have put him up to it.'

The two men looked at each other in amazement. They were struggling to take it all in.

'You girls should be detectives,' Phil said finally.

'That's right,' Pete agreed. 'You've got it all worked out beautifully. The only problem is – it's all wrong.'

'How?' said Holly.

Phil looked at Pete. 'What do you think?' he asked.

Pete shrugged. 'It can't do any harm now. That was the airport police on the phone. They've confirmed it. Shah left for Ireland this morning. The deal must be off.'

'Airport police? What have they got to do with it?'

'Listen,' said Pete. 'You're right. We have been keeping an eye on what's going on at Hanover Hall. But it's not the horse we're interested in. It's Shah.'

172

Something was beginning to stir in Holly's mind. 'It's the smuggling, isn't it?' she said.

'Smuggling?' said Pete. 'What do you know about that?'

'We heard him. He said he'd pay eighty thousand but no more. Then he pulled out altogether.'

'You heard him? When?'

Holly ignored the question. Her mind was working too fast to be held up. 'The smuggling,' she said. 'What is it? Jewellery? Diamonds? We thought it was diamonds.'

Pete shook his head. 'Much more important than diamonds. Tomb relics. Ancient Egyptian tomb relics.'

'Tomb relics?' Belinda was unconvinced. 'Who'd want those?'

'Collectors. Rich collectors, like Shah. We had a tip-off that he was setting up a deal for some items stolen from a Cairo museum. But it looks as though we've wasted our time. The deal's off.

'But it's *not* off,' said Holly. 'There's another collector.'

'The Water Buffalo!' yelled Tracy. 'It's got to be.'

'Of course it is,' grinned Holly. 'Remember the book in his wardrobe. *Tomb Treasures of Ancient Egypt.*' That's why it was there. He must be a collector as well. I knew there had to be some reason he was interested in it.'

'Hold on! Hold on!' Pete tried to slow them down. 'What are you talking about? Water Buffalo?'

'That's just our name for him,' said Tracy. 'He calls himself Crawford,'

'But that's not his proper name,' said Belinda. 'Really he's a film star.'

'Film star?' Phil and Pete looked stunned. 'Mike Barratt!' they said together.

'You know him?' asked Holly.

'We've had our suspicions about him for some time. But we've never been able to prove anything.'

'Well, today's your big day,' said Tracy. 'But there isn't much time. A woman called McLean is bringing the stuff in on this afternoon's ferry from Holland.'

'How do you know?'

'Never mind,' said Holly. 'We've got to get there fast. Let's get down to your van. We'll tell you everything on the way!'

17 Fooled

Getting to the docks before the ferry dropped
anchor was not going to be easy. In the back of
the red van, the members of the Mystery Club were
hurled about from side to side as Pete desperately
tried to save time.

While Pete drove, Phil telephoned ahead to warn
Customs.

'It's a woman called McLean,' he shouted over
the noise of the engine. 'Though she could be
travelling under another name. She's smuggling
objects stolen from a Cairo museum.'

In the back, Holly leaned towards Tracy. 'I only
hope we're right,' she yelled. 'Otherwise we'll be
pretty unpopular.'

'No problem,' shouted Tracy. 'Just as long as we
get there before the ferry docks!'

A moment later, Phil shouted back the good
news. 'They're going to contact the captain and
ask him to track her down before they reach port.
If necessary they'll hold her till we get there.'

'What if she's using a different name?'

'Then you'll have to pick her out. Can you do that?'

'No problem!' Tracy called back. 'Just give me the chance!'

Customs officers were waiting for the van at the dockside.

'The captain's checked the passenger list,' said the officer in charge. 'There's nobody by the name of McLean on board. But don't worry. He's announced that there's going to be a slight delay due to technical problems. That'll give us time to get aboard.'

A small gangplank was already spanning the gap between the ferry and the dockside. Customs officers led the way up, with the Mystery Club and the two policemen in hot pursuit.

On board, the captain was waiting for them. 'I hope this isn't a wild-goose chase,' he said. 'I don't like delaying my passengers for no good reason.'

He showed them to a flight of steps which overlooked the main foot-passenger exit from the ferry. Dozens of passengers were milling around below, waiting to leave the ship.

'Now keep your eyes open,' Pete warned the Mystery Club. 'It's all up to you now.'

The captain gave the order, and the barriers at the top of the gangway were opened. Immediately people began to file forwards.

Tracy scanned the crowds of passengers below.

Her mouth was dry with nerves. So much was resting on her. After all she was the only one to get a good look at the woman. And the only one to hear the conversation about the ferry. If she'd made a mistake this would all turn out to be a waste of time.

Suddenly she gave a yell of excitement.

'That's her!' she said. 'Down there on her own. Carrying the grey bag.'

The chief customs officer put his two-way radio to his lips and gave instructions to his colleagues below. Calmly, without fuss, they moved forward and spoke briefly to McLean. Then they took her gently by the arm and led her towards a sideroom.

The members of the Mystery Club were overjoyed. So were Pete and Phil. Everyone shook hands and clapped each other on the back.

'I hope you're not celebrating too soon,' said the customs officer as he led the way downstairs.

'Don't worry,' said Tracy. 'We're not. It's all going to plan!'

The chief customs officer motioned them to one side. 'You'll have to wait here I'm afraid.' he said as he disappeared into the room where McLean had been taken.

The tension outside was almost unbearable. The Mystery Club was silent. Even the two policemen were pacing backwards and forwards, unable to keep still.

Ten minutes later the door opened and McLean stepped out. She was still carrying her bag. The customs officer was behind her. There was a puzzled look on his face.

'Thank you for your help, madam,' he was saying. 'Sorry for any inconvenience. Purely routine.' He looked towards Pete and Phil and gave a slight shake of the head.

McLean half turned and smiled sweetly at him. 'That's fine, officer,' she said. 'I understand perfectly. Perhaps now I can go ashore?'

The captain moved forward and took charge. 'Yes, madam. This way if you don't mind. I hope you've had a pleasant journey.'

As she walked towards the passenger exit McLean briefly caught sight of the Mystery Club. The smile never wavered. But there was chill recognition in her eyes.

The customs officer was talking to the two policemen in a low voice. 'Nothing. She was completely clean. Checked everything.'

'Are you certain?'

'Positive. Looks like your information was wrong.'

Suddenly everyone was staring at the Mystery Club. It was clear who was going to get the blame for all this!

Holly and Tracy were shattered. They couldn't

believe what had happened. They watched in amazement as McLean shook hands with the captain and stepped on to the gangway. Still unable to believe that she was going free, they ran across to watch her heading down towards the dockside.

Only Belinda seemed unsurprised by the turn of events.

'Of course,' she said, simply, 'if I were trying to smuggle something, I'd get somebody else to carry it for me.'

'Oh, yes?' said Tracy. It was just the sort of thing Belinda would say. 'Like who?'

'I don't know,' replied Belinda. 'Somebody no one would suspect.'

'Wait a minute,' said Holly. She was staring down at the people milling around on the quayside. 'Look there. See!'

She was pointing to a group of Japanese tourists who had just got off the ferry and were uncertain where to go next. Just behind them, at the edge of the crowd, stood a lone figure watching closely as the passengers left the ship.

Holly was jumping around with excitement. 'Don't you see who it is?'

Suddenly Tracy realised. 'Ainsley James!' she yelled. 'It's Ainsley James!'

'Not that radio reporter?' said Belinda.

'Do you know him then?' The captain, who

was still standing close by, had overheard Tracy's shout.

'Yes,' answered Holly. 'We know him. But what's he doing here?'

The captain smiled. 'He's been onboard doing interviews with myself and the crew. Putting a special feature together. Charming man, isn't he?'

'Charming,' Holly agreed. 'And always around at the right time!'

'It's him,' said Tracy. 'It's got to be. It's too much of a coincidence otherwise.'

McLean had reached the bottom of the gangway. For a split second she looked in James's direction. James turned and walked rapidly away. When Holly looked back, McLean was disappearing into the crowd.

Holly grabbed hold of Tracy and Belinda and began dragging them down the gangway.

'Where are we going?' said Belinda.

'After them, of course!' said Holly.

As they headed towards the quayside they heard the policemen shouting after them to go back. But they took no notice.

There were still a lot of people leaving the ferry. Hurrying was impossible. So by the time they were back on dry land any chance of tracking down McLean or James seemed to have disappeared.

'Now what do we do?' Tracy asked despairingly.

'Looks like they've got away,' said Belinda.

'But not for long,' said Holly pushing her way through the crowd. 'After all, we know where they're going, don't we?'

'Are you sure this is the place you want?' the taxi driver asked as he pulled up outside Dock View Wharf.

The warehouse stood alone overlooking the harbour. Once it must have bustled with activity and goods moving constantly in and out. But now it was unused and boarded up. One side of the building was blackened with smoke and the roof was partly burnt out. There were large notices everywhere:

DANGER.
Fire damaged building.
Keep clear.

Holly handed over the fare. 'This is the place,' she said.

The taxi driver shrugged. He wound up the window, swung the car round in the road and drove off.

The Mystery Club waited until the taxi was out of sight, then the girls turned their attention to the warehouse.

'It looks deserted,' said Belinda. 'Think they're here?'

'We'll soon find out,' said Tracy. 'Where do we get in?'

The front entrance was firmly boarded up. If there was a way in it had to be at the back. To the right of the warehouse a section of wooden fencing had been pulled down. That looked like a definite possibility.

The minute Holly, Belinda and Tracy turned the corner they knew they were on the right track. Two cars were parked down the side of the building – a small green Citroën and a dark blue saloon with a missing door mirror.

Holly felt her heartbeat quicken. They were moving into the danger zone.

There were large double doors at both corners of the rear of the building. The first set was firmly secured by a sturdy padlock. But at the opposite corner, the padlock had been wrenched off. And one of the doors was open.

Inside was a set of concrete stairs. Holly turned to the other two and raised her eyebrows slightly. Tracy nodded. Belinda gave a thumbs-up. Holly smiled and led the way up the steps.

At first floor level, doors led into the main warehouse area. Holly inched one of the doors open. The windows were boarded up. It was almost pitch-black inside. And there was a strong smell of stale smoke. Holly listened for a moment. There was total silence. Holly nodded towards the next flight of stairs.

As they climbed higher they began to pick up the sound of voices. Distant at first, but growing louder all the time. By the time they reached the next landing they could make out two voices. A man's and a woman's.

From the landing, a short corridor led to a glass panelled door. The glass was frosted so it was impossible to see inside, but a rectangle of light showed that the room was occupied.

Pressing themselves against the wall the Mystery Club crept towards the door. As they got nearer so the voices became clearer. It was Ainsley James and Janice McLean. And they were in the middle of a blazing row.

'Everything!' James shouted. 'Trying to dope that racehorse almost ruined everything! Why did you do it?'

'To teach Shah a lesson, of course. Nobody messes me about like that.'

'But all it needs is for Hinkley to squeal to the police and they'll be on to us.'

'He'll say nothing,' McLean answered. 'I warned him what would happen if he did.'

'Perhaps he won't. But Benson might. Using some of the money we got from her to bribe Hinkley was just stupid. We were agreed all along.

183

The money from Benson was only to be used to get hold of the Egyptian stuff.'

'All right. What does it matter?' McLean snapped back.'

'It matters because the police have now pulled her in as well. What happens if she tells them we were blackmailing her?'

The Mystery Club's eyes met. So Benson *was* being blackmailed – by James and McLean. No wonder she had acted so strangely. The secret meetings. The sudden changes in behaviour. The large amounts of money. Now it all made sense.

'Don't you worry about Benson,' said McLean. 'She'll keep her mouth tight shut. She'd do any-thing – even go to jail herself – rather than let the police find out where that precious brother of hers is.'

'Is that so? Then if she's not said anything, how do you explain that business on the ferry?'

'Something to do with those three brats, I sup-pose. They've been getting in the way ever since the beginning. Anyway that's not important. We fooled them. Made them look like lying school-girls. Nobody will take any notice of them from now on.'

'You just better be right,' the reporter threatened. Because if they put the police on to me, you'll go down as well. I'll tell them every last thing I know about you.'

'Look, you're worrying about nothing,' replied McLean. She was trying to calm him now. 'It will all be over soon. The actor arrives. We make the swap. Then we're out of here on the next ferry. There's nothing left to go wrong.'

Holly had heard enough. It was time to call in the police. If they could get them there quickly, they would catch McLean and James redhanded. She turned to motion the others back along the corridor. But as she turned a voice rang out.

'Didn't anyone ever tell you it's rude to listen in on other people's conversations?' Mike Barratt's unmistakable silhouette blocked the way back to the stairs. 'I thought I'd seen the last of you three.' There was an unpleasant tone to his voice. 'Well, maybe we can put that right now.'

Tracy took a step towards him.

'I wouldn't try anything stupid,' he warned. He raised his right hand to show that he was carrying an iron bar. 'I've been in enough thrillers to know you never enter a place like this without protection.' He waved the iron bar in front of him. 'Now, who's going to be first?'

18 Chain reaction

'What the hell's going on?' The door to the office opened and light flooded out.

'You've got visitors,' Crawford told McLean. He started to walk along the corridor, viciously swinging the iron bar in front of him.

'OK, we're going,' said Holly. The Mystery Club edged backwards towards the doorway.

'My goodness, it's Holly Adams, isn't it?' said James with mock friendliness. 'Holly and friends. Come in. I hope it doesn't seem rude but I'd rather hoped I'd seen the last of you.'

One by one, McLean grabbed hold of Holly, Belinda and Tracy and pushed them across the room. 'It seems that I underestimated you girls. You're obviously very clever.'

'Too clever for your own good,' said James with a chilling smile. He herded them back into a corner, then pushed a desk in front of them, fencing them in. 'Now we're going to have to deal with you once and for all!'

'I think I'd better warn you. The police are

on their way,' said Holly. 'They'll be here any minute.'

'I should hope so too,' said James. 'Three girls on their own in a very dangerous building. It shouldn't be allowed. It'll be no surprise to anybody when they find you've had a very nasty accident.'

Mike Barratt closed the door. 'Later,' he said. 'What you do with them is nothing to do with me. I'm just here to do business. You've got the goods, have you?'

'Oh, yes, we've got them all right. No thanks to these three.' Ainsley James picked up his tape recorder and placed it on a table in the centre of the room. He flipped off the leather carrying-case and turned over the recorder. He took a coin from his pocket. With the edge of the coin he undid the clips that held the back in place. Taking great care he lifted the panel away. The tape machine's motor had been removed. In its place were thick wadges of cotton wool.

James reached into the packing and took out a necklace. It was made up of a series of green, red and yellow beads. And hanging from it was a silver pendant in the shape of a scarab beetle.

Mike Barratt took a pace forward. 'Ingenious!' he said quietly. 'Who would have thought of looking in there?' Barratt's eyes were fixed longingly on the necklace. Finally, he reached out to touch it. But Ainsley James stopped him.

187

'In good time,' he said. Carefully he replaced it in the cotton wool.

'What about the rest of the things?' Barratt demanded.

'All safely here,' Ainsley James smiled. 'A bracelet. Two rings. A small perfume flask. A carved ivory jar. And of course the necklace. Exactly as promised.'

'Let me see them,' Barratt insisted.

'Not until we've seen the money,' Ainsley James replied. He began fitting the tape recorder back together. 'You do have the money?'

'It's in the car,' said Barratt. 'I thought I'd better make sure we had a deal before bringing it in.'

'Then get it,' said McLean. 'Get it and we can all get out of here.'

'Not all,' Ainsley James said menacingly. 'I've got a can of petrol in the boot. I think it's time this building had another fire. A tragic one this time. With a terrible loss of life. Keep your eyes on these three while we're gone,' he told McLean.

Mike Barratt and Ainsley James left the office together. A few seconds later their footsteps could be heard descending the steps.

'You won't get away with this, you know,' said Tracy.

The woman ignored her.

'Once Benson hears something has happened to us she'll tell the police all about you.'

The woman's eyes flicked towards Tracy. 'Shut up!' she said.

'And you'll be the one that gets it in the neck,' Tracy continued. 'Those two will blame you for everything they can.'

McLean stood up slowly and walked towards Tracy. 'I said, shut up,' she repeated.

Tracy placed her hands on the edge of the desk and leaned towards the woman. 'You must be really stupid, you know. Taking the blame for those men.'

Suddenly McLean snapped. She raised her hand to strike at Tracy. But as she moved forward, Tracy gave a mighty shove and overturned the desk. McLean was knocked backwards on to the floor.

'Let's go!' yelled Tracy.

Holly and Belinda jumped the desk and raced for the stairs. It was only at the end of the corridor that they realised Tracy wasn't with them. They turned to go back but already they could hear footsteps below.

'Tracy! What's wrong?' Belinda yelled.

'Go!' Tracy's voice commanded them. 'Just go!'

Holly grabbed Belinda and dragged her towards the stairs. 'It's too late,' she said. 'We'll have to leave her.'

There was only one way to go. Up. And they went.

*   *   *

Tracy and McLean were struggling on the floor as Ainsley James and Mike Barratt raced back into the office. McLean had grabbed Tracy's foot as she jumped over the desk and brought her crashing to the ground. Tracy had kicked out with all her might but McLean had held on grimly.

Ainsley James grabbed Tracy round the waist and lifted her, kicking and yelling, into the air. 'I thought I told you to keep an eye on them!' he snapped angrily at McLean. In one corner of the room was the door to a store cupboard. 'Open that!' he shouted at Mike Barratt. Barratt did as he was told.

Ainsley James carried Tracy across the room and threw her inside. Barratt slammed the door shut. The two men grabbed the upturned desk and wedged it tightly against the cupboard door. 'That should take care of her,' James said. He helped McLean to her feet. 'Now let's get after the others!'

Holly and Belinda raced up the stairs to the next landing. A set of doors led on to the third floor of the warehouse. A further flight of steps carried on to the top.

Holly made a sudden decision. 'In here.' She pushed Belinda through the doors.

It was much lighter at this level. A large part of the floor above had been burnt out in the fire, allowing light to filter down through the holes in the roof. Rows of metal shelving filled the area. Some were still stacked with smoke-blackened boxes. Others were empty except for a thick layer of dust and ash.

One set of shelves was lying on its side near by. Holly and Belinda dragged it across to block the doorway.

'It won't stop them,' said Holly, 'but it should slow them down a bit.'

Holly led the way through the maze of shelves towards the opposite side of the warehouse. There, doors led on to a second stairway running down that side of the building. It seemed the perfect escape route. But at the first landing the way down was blocked, piled high with a jumble of partly burnt packing-cases. There was no way through.

'Now what?'

Belinda sank down on to the stairs. It looked as though their only chance of escape had disappeared. But Holly refused to give in.

'We'll just have to go up instead,' she said.

She dragged Belinda to her feet and set off back the way they had come. On the next floor, they could hear their pursuers trying to smash their way through the blocked entrance.

As Holly and Belinda stumbled up the last set of stairs the doors below finally gave way. Footsteps began racing backwards and forwards along the aisles of shelves. In a couple of minutes they would realise that the two girls weren't there. Then they would try the stairs.

On the top landing, light was flooding in through a massive hole in the roof, where the fire-fighters had smashed their way in to get to the centre of the blaze. The doors into the warehouse had been torn off their hinges and thrown to one side.

Holly came to a halt in the doorway. She turned to Belinda. 'There's no way across,' she said.

The floor at this level had been badly damaged by the fire. In most of the central area the floorboards had been partly or completely burnt through. There were huge gaps where there were none at all. In other areas the wood was so badly charred that it was unsafe to walk on.

'So what do we do?' said Belinda. 'We can't go back down.'

It was then that Holly noticed the doors in the wall. Large wooden doors, well above floor level, with steps leading up to them. She began tugging at the rusty bolts that held them shut.

'Give me a hand,' she whispered to Belinda.

'What's the point? We must be thirty metres up in the air,' Belinda wailed.

'Maybe it's a fire escape,' said Holly. 'Now, come on.'

With renewed hope Belinda grabbed hold of one of the bolts and wrenched it back. The door flew open, sending her crashing backwards into a pile of chains. 'Well?' she asked as she picked herself up.

Holly was already looking out. 'It's no good,' she said. 'It's not a fire escape.'

'What is it then?'

Holly pointed to the metal framework sticking out from the wall. At the end of it was a pulley system with a chain hanging down.

'It's a loading-bay door. From here they could load and unload direct on to boats below.'

'So there's no way out.'

Holly was staring at the chain hanging down from the pulley. 'No. Unless I can climb down that.'

Belinda grabbed hold of her. 'Don't be stupid! You'd kill yourself.'

'Which would save *us* a job,' said McLean from the top of the stairs. 'Why not try it?'

Tracy had been badly winded when Ainsley James threw her into the store cupboard. But gradually her breathing returned to normal. Or as normal as the situation would allow.

As she recovered, she realised that there was no sound of voices in the office outside. She guessed that everyone had gone looking for Holly and Belinda.

She reached out and pushed at the door. There was no movement at all. A shelf was digging

193

uncomfortably into the small of her back. She placed her hands flat on the shelf and lifted herself up to sit on it. Carefully, she inched backwards in the dark until she felt the pressure of the wall behind her.

Tracy lifted her knees towards her chin and placed the soles of her feet against the door. *Now,* she said to herself, *let's see how much stronger all that time in the weights room has made you.*

She began to push. The door stayed firm. She got her back, thighs and calves direct into line and tried again. There was an almost imperceptible movement. She took a deep breath, held it, and pushed for all she was worth.

Holly took hold of Belinda's arm and began to edge sideways away from the loading-bay doors. It would be the easiest thing in the world for their attackers to push them through there to their deaths below.

McLean, James and Barratt moved menacingly towards them, Mike Barratt brandishing the iron bar threateningly. James and McLean were unarmed. But noticing a length of chain on the floor, James dropped to a squat and grabbed one end.

'You know you can't get away with this,' said Holly.

'On the contrary,' said Ainsley James, looking straight into her eyes. 'Nothing could look more

194

like an accident than the two of you falling through a burnt out floor.'

He swung the chain in a wide arc. It passed within a hand's breadth of Holly's face. She took a step backwards through the doorway into the warehouse. The chain flicked out again. This time Belinda flinched as the end of it whipped past her eyes.

They tried to edge sideways away from James. But as they did so, Mike Barratt stepped forward and blocked the way. Clinging together, Holly and Belinda were driven backwards towards the gaping hole in the floor.

Twice Holly tried to change direction but immediately James or Barratt moved to cut them off, driving them back like lions across a circus cage. Floorboards began to creak and dip underneath their feet. Another metre, less perhaps, and the boards would give way altogether, sending them crashing through to the floor below.

Sliding her foot backwards Holly felt her heel sink into the burnt wood. She stopped. The chain flicked out. The tip of it caught a lock of her hair. She gasped, but she held her ground. James began to swing again. In a long raking arc. But suddenly he caught sight of something on the other side of the warehouse. His arm dropped to his side. His mouth opened in amazement. McLean and Crawford also looked as though they'd just seen a ghost.

'How did you get out?' James finally managed to say.

'Never mind!' It was Tracy, speaking from the opposite doorway. 'The point is I'm here. And I've got something with me. Something you want.' In one hand she carried Ainsley James's tape recorder, in the other a black brief-case.

'Interested in these?' she taunted.

Mike Barratt began to shake. 'She's got everything. The relics and the money.'

McLean was staring wild-eyed at the two men. 'Don't just stand there,' she screamed. 'Do something!'

'I wouldn't,' said Tracy. 'Not unless you want this lot tipped down through the hole in the floor.'

'No!' Ainsley James barked out. 'Don't do that. We can do a deal. You give us those back, and we let your friends go.'

'OK,' said Tracy.

Holly and Belinda began to move towards the safety of the landing. But McLean blocked the way.

'No!' she ordered. 'She's trying to fool us. They stay here until we've got what we want.'

'Got what you want? That could be difficult,' said Tracy.

'What do you mean?' said James.

'I mean I've looked inside the brief-case. Barratt's trying to fool you. Underneath the top layer of notes there are bundles of newspaper.'

196

'What!'

'I don't think there's more than a few thousand pounds there.'

In an instant, McLean and James had forgotten Holly and Belinda and turned their hostility on Barratt instead.

'If this is true, Mr Film Star,' James snarled, 'you're going to regret it for the rest of your life!'

Barratt was mystified. 'I don't know what she's talking about,' he insisted. 'She's lying!'

But seeds of doubt had been sown, and Tracy wasn't finished. 'It doesn't matter anyway,' she shouted across. 'A few thousand pounds is much more than these trinkets are worth.'

It was Barratt's turn to be suspicious. 'Trinkets?' he repeated.

Tracy laughed. 'You don't really think a couple of two-bit crooks like these could get hold of the genuine articles? These are fakes.'

'I – I don't believe you,' Mike Barratt stammered.

'Oh, no?' said Tracy. 'Why do you think they wouldn't let you have a closer look at them?'

'She's bluffing. Don't listen to her,' said McLean.

But Barratt's suspicions had been aroused. 'Is it true?' he demanded. 'Is it?'

'Of course it's true!' shouted Tracy. 'If you don't believe me. See for yourself.'

With two rapid movements, she sent first the

brief-case and then the tape recorder flying over the gap in the floor on to the blackened boards opposite. In a frenzy, Ainsley James and Mike Barratt dived forward to grab them. But as they did so, the weakened flooring disintegrated. In a cloud of dust and ash the two men crashed through to the floor below, taking the tape recorder and brief-case with them.

At the edge of the gaping hole, Janice McLean stood frozen with horror, staring blindly down at the shattered floorboards. She was still there five minutes later when the police and ambulance arrived.

'I was stupid. I should have told the police straight away.'

Benson and the Mystery Club were sitting in an interview room at the Willow Dale police station.

'I just thought that if I gave them the money they'd leave me alone.'

'Blackmailers never leave you alone,' said Belinda. 'They just keep coming back for more.'

Benson swirled the remains of her coffee round and round in the bottom of the polystyrene cup. 'You're right, of course,' she sighed. 'They were bound to track me down in the end.'

As soon as Benson had heard about the events at the warehouse, she had told the police everything she knew. How she had desperately tried to avoid the blackmailers. How they had finally caught up with her that night at the restaurant. And how they had threatened to let the police know where to find her brother unless she paid them thirty thousand pounds.

Holly put her arm around the writer's shoulders. 'You don't have to worry,' she told her. 'The police are bound to release you now they know you were being blackmailed.'

'It's not me I'm worried about,' said Benson. 'It's my brother John.'

'Look, maybe I'm stupid,' Tracy admitted. 'But I still don't see how he fits into all this.'

Benson crushed the cup and threw it into the bin. 'It started about fifteen years ago. John met Janice McLean in a pub. They became friends and set up in business together. Some sort of property company. After about twelve months they went broke, owing a lot of people a lot of money. McLean came to me and told me that she'd discovered that the police were going to arrest them for fraud. She said if I gave her ten thousand pounds they could escape and start a new life in Spain. I knew it was wrong. But I couldn't stand the thought of John going to jail.'

'Did he admit he'd done it?' Holly asked.

'He had no head for business. He simply didn't understand how it had all happened. But his signature was on the papers. That made him responsible.'

'So you're saying that your brother and McLean went to Spain together?' Tracy was still struggling to sort it all out.

'That's right. The Costa del Sol. After a couple of years McLean walked out on him. Just disappeared. Never heard anything else about her. Until that day in the hotel.'

'No wonder you were so shocked when Ainsley James suddenly mentioned her name,' said Holly.

Benson's head dropped forward. She stared down at her hands resting in her lap. 'It was like a bolt out of the blue,' she said eventually. 'A nightmare come to life. And it's continued ever since.'

'But it's over now.' Holly tried to comfort her. 'It's all out in the open. There's nothing to be afraid of any more.'

'But what's going to happen to John now the police know where he is?' asked Benson. 'That's what bothers me.'

The door to the interview room flew open and Pete and Phil the two police officers walked in. They were looking particularly pleased with themselves.

'Right, Miss Benson, you can go,' Phil smiled. 'McLean's admitted everything.'

There was a silence. Benson barely moved. The smile disappeared from the policeman's face.

'I thought I was giving you good news,' he said gently. 'Is something wrong?'

'My brother. What are you going to do about him?'

Pete took over. 'You don't understand. McLean has told us all about it. The blackmail, the smuggling, the horse-doping and the fraud. It was all down to her. She's admitted that your brother never knew anything about it. She'd fooled him just like she fooled everybody else.'

For a moment, Benson seemed unable to take it all in. 'Are you telling me he's got nothing to fear?' she said slowly.

'Nothing at all. The only ones with anything to worry about are McLean, James and Barratt. And if that shelving hadn't broken their fall James and Barratt wouldn't be around to go to jail. And that would be a great pity.'

'Of course,' Phil continued, 'they came very close to getting away with it. In fact, if it hadn't been for these three here, it could all have been very different.'

Benson stood up. 'That's very true,' she said. All her tiredness had suddenly disappeared. It was as though a great weight had been lifted from her shoulders. 'You know,' she said, looking at the Mystery Club, 'I think I would like to buy you girls the biggest and best ice-creams you have ever had in your lives.'

'You're on,' said Belinda, jumping to her feet.

'And while we're eating,' Benson continued, 'we are going to talk about what I can do to thank you for sorting all this out.'

'I think we're already decided that, haven't we?' Holly asked the others.

'We have,' Tracy and Belinda agreed.

'What is it then?' asked the writer.

'Dedicate your next book to us.'

'I'll do it,' said Benson. 'It'll read "With thanks to Holly, Tracy and Belinda. My friends in the Mystery Club".'

TITLES AVAILABLE IN THE MYSTERY CLUB SERIES

All these books are available at your local bookshop or newsagent or can be ordered direct from the publisher. Just tick the titles you want and fill in the form below.

Prices and availability subject to change without notice.

HODDER AND STOUGHTON PAPERBACKS, PO Box 11, Falmouth, Cornwall.

Please send cheque or postal order for the value of the book, and add the following for postage and packing.
UK including BFPO – £1.00 for the book, plus 50p for the second book, and 30p for each additional book ordered up to a £3.00 maximum.
OVERSEAS INCLUDING EIRE – £2.00 for the first book, plus £1.00 for the second book and 50p for each additional book ordered.
OR Please direct debit this amount from my Access/Visa Card (delete as appropriate).

Card Number

Amount £ ....

Expiry Date ....

Signed ....

Name ....

Address ....